BEFORE THE DAWN: BOOK NINE OF BEYOND THESE WALLS

A POST-APOCALYPTIC SURVIVAL THRILLER

MICHAEL ROBERTSON

EDITED AND COVER BY ...

To contact Michael, please email:
subscribers@michaelrobertson.co.uk

Edited by:

Pauline Nolet - http://www.paulinenolet.com

Cover design by Dusty Crosley - https://www.deviantart.com/dustycrosley

COPYRIGHT

Before the Dawn: Book nine of Beyond These Walls

Michael Robertson
© Michael Robertson 2021

Before the Dawn: Book nine of Beyond These Walls is a work of fiction. The characters, incidents, situations, and all dialogue are entirely a product of the author's imagination, or are used fictitiously and are not in any way representative of real people, places, or things.

Any resemblance to persons living or dead is entirely coincidental.

All rights reserved.

No part of this publication may be reproduced, stored in a retrieval system, or transmitted in any form or by any means electronic, mechanical, photocopying, recording, or otherwise, without the prior written permission of the author except in the case of brief quotations embodied in critical articles and reviews.

READER GROUP

Join my reader group for all my latest releases and special offers. You'll also receive these four FREE books. You can unsubscribe at any time.

Go to - www.michaelrobertson.co.uk

BEFORE THE DAWN: BOOK NINE OF BEYOND THESE WAL...

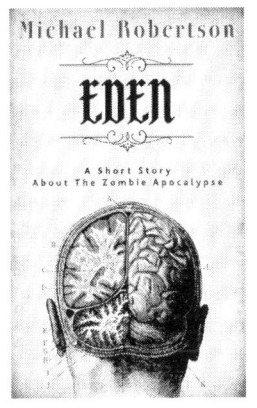

CHAPTER 1

They all had their strengths. William had many. He could fight. He could run. He could be the diplomat of the group and keep everything moving in the right direction. But he couldn't throw a spear for shit. He could, however, shelve his ego and recognise when to let the others take the lead. The heavy steel sword he'd brought from Gracie's community in a tight grip, he stood back while Gracie, Artan, and Hawk acted as their first line of defence.

Thwip! Artan, the most skilled of the three, moved with machine efficiency. His arm a piston, he threw one spear after the other, each one landing true and taking down another attacking diseased.

Thwip! Gracie hit a diseased woman in her left eye, burying the flint tip into her socket with a *squelch!*

Thwip! Hawk missed and stood aside. William filled the gap and silenced the screaming man by ramming the tip of his sword into his mouth so hard it punched through the back of his head.

As the creature fell, William unsheathed his sword from

its throat and spun away so it didn't take his weapon with its clumsy fall.

Thwip! This time, Hawk nailed a creature through the neck.

Olga spotted for Artan, which gave her the least to do.

Matilda, who stood behind Gracie, finished the last of the diseased, driving her sword into the side of its head. She penetrated its skull with a *pop!*

William reached across and held Matilda's hand. He fought to control his breaths. "You okay?"

A slight smile, Matilda dipped a gentle nod. "Yeah. It's nothing we haven't done before, right?"

The ground was littered with fallen diseased. Olga's cheeks bulged with her exhale. "It might take a while for Max to get his head around coming outside again."

"This is nothing," Gracie said. "Sometimes there are hundreds of them out here. And the diseased are the least of our worries."

Max, who still hadn't gotten his head straight from his time in the asylum, had remained back at Dout. Dianna had too. "He'll need a few days, eh?" William said.

Olga leaned closer to William. "And then some."

They'd been climbing a steep hill, the grass up to their knees. Always harder fighting the creatures while ascending, but like Matilda had said; nothing they hadn't done before.

While retrieving several of her spears and sliding them into the holder on her back, Gracie said, "You all ready to keep going?"

William nodded.

The top of the wall had been visible before they'd begun their ascent. The massive steel structure formed its own gunmetal grey horizon. Made from the same rough steel as the funnel, it might have stood so tall no one could see over it, but, on first impressions, it hadn't appeared to be as impressive as the fun—

"Oh my," Matilda said.

William halted next to her on the brow of the hill. The wind rocked him where he stood. Spring brought a freshness and warmth, but at this height, the strong gales still chewed through his thin layers. "You can say that again." The other side of the hill fell away from them. Had it been much steeper, it would have been a cliff edge. It revealed the bottom ninety percent of the gigantic wall about one thousand feet away. One hundred and fifty to two hundred feet tall. At least. "How the hell—"

"Are you supposed to get past that?" Gracie said.

"Yeah."

Gracie shrugged. "I wish I could offer some insight."

William's top flapped in the wind. "It looks like something from another world. Like it doesn't belong here, you know?" He looked up at the clear blue sky. "Almost as if an alien species dropped it and left."

Rummaging around in her bag, Gracie pulled out a pair of tubes with glass discs covering each end and passed them to William.

They were light to hold and fitted in the palm of his hand. "What are these?"

"Binoculars." She pulled out another set and held them up to her eyes. "You look through them."

William copied Gracie and stumbled backward when the wall jumped closer. "Jeez!" He pulled them away, blinked several times, and raised them again. "Wow."

"We want you to see what you're up against. Those lumps running along the top of the wall are sentry guns."

Twin barrels protruded from large grey mounds. They were about twenty feet apart and stretched away to either side, vanishing from sight.

"They're like the guns on the bottom of the drones," Gracie said. "They're automatic. They sense motion and shoot. If you try to climb over the wall, they'll rip you to shreds."

Olga snorted. "Like we can climb over that."

In any other situation, William's attention would have fallen on the diseased first. Until now, they'd always been the greatest threat to their lives. But they were separated by a hill too steep for the creatures to climb, so what danger did the diseased really pose? Gathered outside the wall, the creatures milled about in small packs. They stumbled through the long grass, screaming, slashing at the air, snarling at invisible enemies. Some of them fell over, the co-ordination required to remain upright having left with their humanity.

William pressed the binoculars to his eyes again and followed the line of the wall to the left and the right. "It really doesn't end."

"You thought we were lying?" Gracie said.

"No. But I still found it hard to believe." He handed his binoculars to Matilda while Gracie passed hers to Artan.

"This is the only part of the wall that has gates," Gracie said.

The gates were flush with the rest of the impenetrable steel barricade. Invisible save for their outline. They were about forty feet square with a vertical line down their centre.

"So we go around," Matilda said.

Gracie shook her head and held her hand out to William. "Can I have your map?"

Crumpled from where he'd carried it in his back pocket, William unfolded the map in the strong wind and handed it to Gracie.

She hunched down, flattened the long grass, and spread the map for them all to see. She ran her finger along the thick line bisecting the depicted land. "This wall runs from coast to coast. The only way around is if you swim. And then you have to swim for miles because the wall runs down both coastlines. You're more vulnerable in the water than anywhere else. There's nowhere to hide. The chances are you'll get shot before you get your hair wet."

"Then we have to work out how to climb it," William said.

"Maybe," Gracie said. "If I knew anyone who'd made it over, I'd tell you how they did it."

"That doesn't mean it hasn't been done." William picked up the map before the wind carried it away. "It's not like someone would risk everything to get over the wall and then come back to tell you how they did it."

"That's true."

"Okay, we get it." Matilda swiped her hair back and held it in place on the top of her head. "It won't be easy. But will it be worth it?"

Gracie shrugged. "Who knows? It's like William said, no one's ever returned to talk about it."

Olga handed her binoculars back to Gracie. "Why don't they kill the diseased?"

Gracie opened her mouth, but a loud tone wailed across the landscape, cutting her off. Several hundred diseased below them, every one of them turned to face the wall and took off towards its gates. There were two mounds on top of the wall that weren't sentry guns. Directly above the gates, each had a spinning light housed in red glass.

Having only just recovered from the climb, William's lungs tightened again. "What's that noise? What's going on?"

Gracie looked over each shoulder. "We need to get out of here."

"Why?" William said.

Clack! The line running down the centre of the gates parted, darkening where it opened by a few inches. The initial clack repeated until it morphed into a continuous drone of turning cogs accompanied by the *whoosh* of steel chains in motion. It took William back to leaving the national service area. The massive wooden gates. A line of protectors ahead of them. Everything had been so new then. His heart overflowed with hope. The great Edin dream. You can make it if you work hard enough. The gap grew larger; the gates opening outwards, away from the wall.

"Come on." Gracie tugged on William's arm. "We need to go."

"What if this gives us a clue how we might get through to the other side?"

Another check over each shoulder, Gracie's cheeks flushed. She bounced on the spot and chewed the inside of her mouth. "I want you to promise me something."

William shrugged.

"If we stay longer, the next time I say we have to go, we go, okay? We can push this as far as is safe so you can see more, but I need you to promise me you'll trust me when I say we're out of time."

William nodded. As did Artan, Matilda, and Hawk. Olga remained tight-lipped. Things might have gotten better between the two girls, but they most certainly weren't at a point where Gracie told Olga what to do.

The wild call of a diseased horde fifty feet to their left. Shrill. Strained. Rabid. About forty of them in total. Men, women, and children. They slashed at the air, and the grass swished against their legs. They crested the hill and charged down the other side. Several tripped. One of them landed face first, its cheek planting on the ground while its legs sailed over the top of its head. *Crack!* It fell limp with its breaking neck. The others trampled it on their way down. They joined the masses closing in on the opening gates.

Another pack on their right. Farther away than those on their left, and about twice as many in the group.

Gracie continued to turn one way and then the other. She continued to bounce on the spot.

"We still good?" William said.

"As long as you run when I say."

"How many diseased do they call to the gates?"

"It's not the diseased you need to worry about." She looked over her shoulders again.

The cogs cackled. The gap down the centre of the gates grew wider. "That has to be our way in," William said.

Gracie shook her head. "I wouldn't be so sure."

A person ran from the gates. Tiny because of how far away they were. They sprinted. Their arms pumped. They dodged the diseased closing in on all sides.

"It's like Edin," Matilda said.

The trips to the back wall with his dad … William's eyes itched. He flinched and then relaxed at Matilda's gentle touch on his back.

A diseased slammed into the runner. They knocked heads, and both turned flaccid. Another diseased pounced on the unconscious person. A wild animal on its prey, it pulled away from its first bite. William winced at the blood spraying from the escapee's throat.

More people spilled from the opening gates. One in every two were taken down within the first ten feet. The more nimble found their way through parts of the crowd. Very few got all the way clear.

"This is what we call the estuary," Gracie said. "This is why they don't kill the diseased."

Olga tutted. "Stop talking in riddles."

"She isn't," Artan said. "An estuary is the start of a river. As in, this is where all the diseased in the north come from. Whoever's responsible for opening the gates seem to be doing it, in part at least, to make sure there are always diseased in the north."

Olga turned to Gracie. "Is that right? *All* of them come from here?"

"Yeah." Gracie nodded. She turned to Hawk. "This is why, no matter how hard you fight, you'll *never* beat the diseased. You can spend the rest of your life killing them, but there will *always* be more."

More and more escapees ran from the prison gates. Small groups of diseased broke away from the main pack as they chased the people making bids for freedom. William said, "How many people do they let out at a time?"

"Sometimes hundreds," Gracie said. She checked their surroundings again.

Escapee after escapee came to bloody and violent ends. William's stomach churned. Bile lifted into his throat. "How often do they do this?"

Gracie's long plait swung from her continued checks. "If they have a set time or schedule, we don't know it. They open the gates more during the day than at night. They do it regularly enough I was confident I'd be able to show it to you at some point. I think this is the best way to understand what this place is about."

"So," William said, "the wall has no weak spots?"

"I'm sure it does. I just can't tell you what they are."

William had partly folded the map when he'd picked it up from the ground, but it still flapped in the wind. He released his grip, and it took off on the breeze. "I don't suppose that will be much use where we're going."

"So you're still going to try?" Gracie said.

"Whatever's happening down there"—William pointed at the gates—"there has to be a way past it. I need to see what's on the other side of the wall. You've heard the stories of how great it is in the south. Besides, we've come too far to give up now."

"But what if they're just that? Stor—" A snarling to their left cut Gracie short.

"That doesn't sound like the diseased," William said.

"We have to go. Now!" Gracie took off, jogging back the way they came.

Every step slammed through William with his clumsy descent. His feet twisted on the uneven ground. If he fell, he'd break an ankle, but he had to keep up with Gracie. He'd insisted on staying; now he had to make good on his promise.

"Down!" Gracie dropped into a hunch.

William followed the others, slamming onto his knees while pulling his head lower than the long grass.

A group of men and women appeared at the bottom of the hill. Twenty to thirty of them, they had as many snarling dogs. They spoke to one another in a language William didn't understand. Maybe the same language as the woman who'd appeared while they were on national service.

The group were about forty feet away, the wailing alarm on the other side of the hill calling to them like it called the diseased.

"Jeez," Gracie said. Her usually pale face had turned puce and glistened with sweat. "Were they any closer, those dogs would have sniffed us out. We should have moved on sooner." The dogs and people vanished over the brow of the hill. "That's why I said the diseased weren't the things to worry about."

"But why do we need to worry about those people?" Hawk said. "They're like us."

A shake of her head, Gracie lost focus as she stared into the middle distance. "They're *nothing* like us. And if you think that, you won't last long around here."

Olga threw a shrug in Gracie's direction. "So who are they?"

A hare checking for danger, Gracie poked her head above the long grass. "You'll find out soon enough. Now let's go."

They reached the bottom of the hill, the wailing siren and diseased massacre now muted because of the distance between them. Gracie slowed their pace.

"Olga," William said, "how's Max doing?"

Olga's lips tightened. She raised her eyebrows.

"You think he might help us get through those gates?"

"Right now?" She shook her head. "I think we'll have a hard time just trying to persuade him to leave his room."

CHAPTER 2

Max shouldn't have come here. But what else could he do? Lie in bed all day with a rumbling stomach? And the more time he spent alone in his room, the harder it would be to come out again. No, he'd done the right thing. Whatever happened, he needed to remain connected to people and the world around him. Because if he didn't, the black hole in his mind would surely consume him.

The steel tabletop was cold against his forearms. The hard surface uncomfortable to lean on, but the chill kept him grounded. It kept him in the moment. A small plate to one side. A dirty knife and fork lay across it. Flakes of pastry covered the white ceramic and the surrounding tabletop. The meat from the pasty left a gamey taste in his mouth, and the high concentration of salt had dried his tongue and throat. A thirst his mint tea couldn't sate. Still, he took another sip, his lips tingling from the heat. The place empty for now, he should just get a cup of water. But what if people came in? He shouldn't have come here. One of his friends would have brought him food to the room had he waited.

The dining tables ran across the long hall in uniform

lines. Made from the same steel as the walls, floor, and ceiling. Equidistant, their parallel surfaces stretched away from him. They showed just how far he had to travel to get out of there. Why had he chosen this seat in the first place? The lights stung his tired eyes. He blinked repeatedly and rubbed them, but it only heightened the discomfort. The same burning tingle on his lips gave him pins and needles in his palms. The mug in his grip all the hotter compared to the chilled tabletop. He clenched his jaw. He bounced his right leg, spending his nervous energy. If only he could turn it into the action required to leave. He shouldn't have come here.

At least he'd found a corner. In a large open room filled with rows of tables, he'd claimed a relatively private space. Albeit about as far away from the door as he could possibly be. A wall to his left and behind him. Maybe a table reserved for those with more privilege, but with no one else around, how could anyone tell him where to sit?

Laughter fired into the room, and Max flinched. It bounced off the hard walls and rattled around inside his skull. The people who made up the group were all in their mid to late twenties. A mix of men and women. Ten to fifteen of them in total. Each one of their voices stabbed a different needle into his brain. They crossed the room to the serving area where he'd grabbed his pasty.

One by one, they fell silent. One by one, they stared at Max.

Max gripped his mug tighter. The tips of his fingers turned white.

One woman in the group halted, pinned by Max's glare. Her cheeks reddened, but she grinned through her discomfort. She had curly black hair and a brilliant white smile. She turned away and pulled on the arms of some of the men. Their egos needed a helping hand with ignoring the staring Max. They returned to getting their food and taking their seats at one of the long tables. Other than the occasional glance, they got stuck into their food.

Crash!

Max jumped and yelled. His cry echoed through the dining hall long after the sound of the dropped pan from the kitchen had faded.

"What the fuck?" one man at the table said. From the way he held himself—shoulders squared, chin raised, eyes sharp, looking for trouble—he had the largest ego in the group. In his mid to late twenties, he'd already gone bald. Maybe that explained his demeanour. A tight crop around the back and sides, the light bounced off his glistening pate. He raised an eyebrow, his lip arching beneath it.

The man's stare glazed with blood. His mouth opened and closed. He worked his jaw as if stretching out an ache. He bit at the air, tasting the space between them. A gash opened on his cheek. It unzipped from the top down, the flesh turning outwards from the putrid wound.

Max squirmed where he sat, his palms damp with sweat.

The man's head caved in from the right. A slow crumpling of his skull, a collapsing of his head's structure like a failing wet paper mache bust. One of his eyes protruded from its socket before it fell and dragged a line of clotted blood down his pallid cheek. It hung from its small bloody rope.

The man continued to stare at Max while his head leaned to one side. It bent at the neck until it cracked like a snapping flower stem.

Sweat ran into Max's already burning eyes.

"Gary!" The same woman who'd previously pulled the men away. "Gary!" She tugged on his arm.

His heart in his throat, Max dropped his focus to the gunmetal grey tabletop.

Wedged in the corner. The table cold. The mug scalding. His mind ran laps. *Mad Max.*

A shake of his head to dislodge the words. "No!"

Crash! Another pan hit the floor in the kitchen. An angry man yelled, "What the fuck are you doing?"

A boy replied, "I'm sorry."

"Stop being so clumsy, you—"

The man's yell morphed into a snarl. The boy offered a gargled response. An argument between two enraged diseased.

Max let go of his mug of tea and grabbed his knife and fork.

The screaming and snarling grew louder. Thirty creatures charged from their prison cells into the Asylum's dark corridors. They came forward in a wave, tripping over one another to get to him.

Max stood up and backed into the corner. The narrow hallway funnelled the creatures' charge. Waiting for the right moment, he drove his fork deep into the eye of the first diseased. The prongs hit the inside of the back of its skull. He removed it with a deep *squelch* and drew out a line of blood that soaked the table.

More diseased, Max's arms moved like pistons, stabbing one and then the next. For every fallen creature, two replaced it. They climbed over the growing mound of corpses to get to him.

The next diseased got too close to stab. Max held it back with shaking arms. It bit at the air between them. Black ichor stretched across its diseased lips as a thick webbing. Its snapping teeth came together with castanet clicks. Max maintained his grip on its shoulders and squeezed. The only defence he had; the thing bit and bit and bit. *Click! Click! Click!*

Something tapped Max's forehead. The contact hit him in time with the diseased's snapping teeth. *Click! Click! Click!* Tap. Tap. Tap. The diseased vanished. The diseased and its mound of dead friends. The small cherubic face of a little girl replaced it. She was about six years old. They were back in the dining hall. The chefs shouted at one another in the kitchen. The table of twenty-somethings chatted and ate together.

The girl in front of him continued tapping his forehead. She had tight curly blonde hair, brown eyes, and a round face. She smiled. "Are you okay, mister?" Every time she said *mister,* she tapped his forehead again. A pecking bird. "Mister? Mister? Mister?"

Max crushed the desire to snap her finger by tightening his grip on his fork. He dodged her next attack. "Will you *stop* that?"

"Sorry, mister. Are you okay?"

"I'm fine—" his chest so tight he had to pause for breath "—thank you."

"You don't look fine. You look unwell. Shall I call my mummy?"

"No!" Max shook his head.

"In fact," the girl said, sliding into his personal space, "I'd say you look extremely unwell." She shifted closer again, so close her body heat pushed against him. He shuffled left by an inch before he hit the wall. He could hardly shove her back.

"Mister?"

Her face changed. Her *mister* morphed into a phlegmy syllable. A primordial growl. Several of her teeth spilled from her mouth. One of them stuck to her bottom lip, tacky with black goo. Blood glazed her eyes. Max pushed against the wall as if he might somehow phase through it.

The girl's face returned. She held her head with a curious

tilt. Max winced. The lights in the dining hall were too bright.

"Mister?"

The girl's high-pitched voice drilled into him. Her appearance fluctuated between diseased and cherub. Diseased and cherub.

"What do you want?" Max's voice rang through the dining hall.

The girl moved back by a few inches. "I said you look unwell. That I should help. Mummy said I should always help people in need. You look like someone in need. Are you someone in need, mister?"

He *needed* to get out of there. To get back to his room and get his head together. He could later blame it on a fever. Although, a fever in a place like this ... would they kick him out? What did they do to disease carriers in such an enclosed space? He couldn't risk being sent outside. He could say the rich meat didn't agree with him. Not a fever. Not a virus. Something he ate. Something no one else could catch.

"Mister?"

Back on national service. In the hall where they'd done much of their training. The one with the glass wall behind the curtains that gave them a view into the two holding cells. The girl joined him in the hall. She stood in one cell, and he stood in the other. She stood where the sheep had been. He stood in the cell that had been occupied by the diseased.

The sheep bleated, "Mister? Mister?"

The separating wall between them lifted.

The sheep continued, "Mister? Mister?"

Dropping to its front, the diseased reached beneath the wall. *He* reached beneath the wall, stretching his long, atrophied arm beneath the gap, clawing in the girl's direction. In the sheep's direction.

"Mister."

In the dining hall again. Max pulled his hand back. He held his knife and fork to his chest.

The sheep bleated. "Mister."

Another kid appeared. A boy. Eight or nine years old. He had a long face, greasy hair, and a big nose. He'd brought friends with him.

"Tell us about where you've been, mister. What's it like outside, mister?"

The separating wall between the diseased and the sheep lifted higher. Max stretched his head under. He bit at the air, snapping in the sheep's direction.

It continued bleating. "Mister. Mister. Mister."

There were now about ten kids in the dining hall. The eight-year-old boy rested on the table and leaned over Max. He had deep gashes on the backs of his hands that were filled with black tar and maggots.

The kids closed in and blocked his exit.

"Did you see many diseased?"

"Where did you come from?"

"What's the north like?"

"Mister?"

"Mister?"

"Baaaaaa."

The crew of small diseased stared at Max. There were no kids here. They loosed a phlegmy rattle. An indecipherable snarl. Snapping jaws. They closed in tighter.

"Yeargh!" Max yelled and brought his fork over in a wide arc. He buried it into the skull of the eight-year-old. The kid fell, and Max kicked its foetid little body away. He swung for the next diseased freak with his knife and tore its cheek open. He drove his fork into a small beast's eye. They were easier to fight off at this size.

The table of twenty-somethings stared at him. All of them diseased. All of them waiting for their chance to pounce.

Max worked through the kids and kicked the last of the smaller diseased away. He clambered over the pile of child bodies and ran at the table of twenty-somethings. As one, they withdrew from his wild charge. He sprinted from the room, whacking his right shoulder on the door frame as he stumbled into the hallway.

Tired legs, Max ran at the edge of his balance back toward his dorm. He needed a better weapon to end these diseased freaks.

Crack! Max slammed his hand against the button to open his bedroom door and fell into the room. He charged to his bed and grabbed his baton. He turned back to the door and stopped. The room dark. The only sound his own ragged breaths.

"Shit!" Max's stomach sank. Butterflies whipped up a storm of nausea in his guts. "What the fuck have I just done?" He dropped his baton. It hit the steel floor with a *clang*.

Max crawled into his bed and curled into the foetal position. His right shoulder throbbed from where he'd whacked it on the door frame. He trembled and shook his head. "What have I done? What have I done? What have I done? I just want this to end. Take me now. Switch me off." He knocked against his head with his fist. "Just fucking end this!"

The thud of steps against steel outside. An army of boots closed in on his room. What were they going to do to him? Whatever they decided, let it be quick.

The army drew closer. The steps grew louder.

Thud.
Thud.
Thud.

CHAPTER 3

Artan stood aside while William climbed into the hatch. He checked behind again. The fading light gave the diseased more places to hide. The diseased and the gangs with their dogs.

Matilda climbed through the hatch next. The *tock* of her steps against the ladder joined the sound of William's descent.

Who were the people with the dogs, and what drew them to the wall when the siren sounded?

Gracie held the hatch open. They'd attached rubble to its top so when closed, it blended in with the ruined landscape. It sat amongst the wreckage of a crumbling building like it belonged. Had Gracie not lifted it open for them, Artan would have walked straight past it. The roof of the building had fallen in a long time ago, and while the walls stood tall, they'd been much taller in the past. Their tops were uneven from their entropic demise. This building's spire remained intact. It stood over fifty feet tall and gave the best sign of the building's original size. "What did you say this place used to be?"

"A church."

A chill snapped through Artan. "It gives me the creeps."

Gracie flashed a facetious smile. "Even more of a reason to hurry." She flicked her head toward the open hatch.

"Sorry." Artan sat at the edge of the hole and hung his legs down. He swung his foot, feeling for a ladder rung.

Gracie backed in after him, climbing down and slowly lowering the hatch with her. Let that thing slam, and if they weren't being watched when they entered the church's ruins, people would be looking for them after that. One mistake could blow this community's cover.

The long steel-walled tunnel sat thirty feet below the surface. It stretched away from them. Artan waited with William, Matilda, Hawk, and Olga for Gracie to reach the bottom and take the lead. Their steps echoed, and the water in the bladders strapped to their backs swished. They'd stopped at a river on the way home to fill up. Whenever possible, you brought water back for the community. Provide more than you used, and you'd always be welcome.

Brown rectangular cuboids no larger than one of his shoes ran along to the top of each wall where they met the ceiling. One on each side about every twenty feet. Artan pointed at them. "What are they?"

"Explosives," Gracie said.

"They're what?" Hawk's response ran away from him down the tunnel.

Gracie pointed at the next pair of explosives as they passed them. "In a worst-case scenario, we can section the tunnel off …" She walked about another fifteen feet before she pointed at two doors that were flush with the wall. They were embedded in sleeves. "We can close these doors and blow this section. We have the same in each of the eight tunnels. If anyone tries to attack us, they'll get buried beneath tonnes of earth, steel, and whatever else is above them."

"You only have them in the end sections?" Artan said.

Gracie nodded. "Yes. In about the final third of each tunnel."

"And no one's ever set them off by accident?" William said.

"No." Gracie pointed back toward the hidden doors. "There are two keyholes by the doors. You need two people to turn them at the same time to trigger the explosion. Believe me—" she laughed "—this underground living, while safe, isn't for everyone. We've had one or two people go loco over the years, which is why we never give that power to just one person."

Matilda finally spoke. "And you've never had to blow them up?"

"No," Gracie said. "Not yet."

Artan's legs ached, his tired steps slamming down one after the other. "Do you ever get fed up with this long walk?"

"All the time." Gracie rolled her eyes. "The more I do it, the longer it feels. But the length has saved us on more than one occasion. We've had a few people get bitten and still get back into the community. They've all turned by the time they've reached the locked door at the end."

A set of double doors up ahead, a small window a foot square in each one. Gracie knocked seven times.

Unlike when they first came here, no one answered.

Gracie knocked again. "In the evening, just two guards watch the eight doors."

Whoosh! The doors parted, revealing an older woman with white hair. She had leathery skin and brilliant blue eyes. They shone with a vibrancy that belied her age. Her smile changed her demeanour as if her entire body grinned. She threw her arms around Gracie and kissed her cheek. "Good to see you, sweetheart."

"You too, Jane." Gracie stood aside to let the others in. "We expect the guards to check everyone who comes back for bites or any sign of them turning. They don't do it if you're with me, Aus, or Dad. We would have picked it up before this point."

Artan walked through last, Gracie closing the door behind him with another *whoosh!*

Jane smiled at the others like she had Gracie. A hiss of static burst from her right breast and forced Artan back a step.

Still smiling, Jane tapped the black box attached to her jacket. "These are walkie-talkies. They allow us to communicate with one another." She gave him a demonstration, cutting off the static by pressing a button on the side of the box. She leaned towards the device and said, "Dom, I've just let Gracie and her guests in. Everything okay on your side?"

Another sharp static hiss. A man's voice came through. "Yep, everything's good."

Jane might have had an infectious smile that had put most of the group at ease, but Olga still stood tense. The same frown she'd worn for weeks, she said, "So how do you know when to blow up the tunnels? I mean"—she pointed at the window in the closed door behind them—"if you have to wait for someone to get to that window, surely it's too late to stop them coming in by then."

"We have cameras like the one that showed me I needed to return to the ruined city to meet you lot. Come on." Gracie waved for them to follow her. "Let me show you the surveillance room."

Artan, still at the back of the group, gasped when he entered the room. It had the same steel floors and walls. Similar etchings decorated it like the rest of Dout's interior.

But the place glowed with an ethereal blue light projected by a bank of monitors. Each one showed a different scene. Tunnels. The exits from the community, which had diseased near almost every one. The dining hall.

"What the fuck?" Olga said. "Are you watching us the entire time? What kind of sick place is this?"

"We're watching the community, Olga." Gracie nodded at the man who'd been in the room keeping an eye on the monitors. He left. "We have to know if there are any problems that need addressing. The sooner we find that out, the better. And before you ask, we don't watch the bedrooms or bathrooms.

"Also …" Gracie walked over to a wall with several doors. She slid her spear holder from her back and opened a door to reveal hundreds of spears like her own. She placed her weapons inside. "This is the armoury. We keep all our weapons in here. And I have to ask you to hand over yours. It makes people uneasy if anyone's walking around armed. We have enough early warning systems in place, and someone's always on guard to give us the time we need to arm up."

"How do you know you have enough time if it's never happened?" Olga said.

Artan handed over his spears, and Hawk did the same. William and Matilda handed Gracie their swords. Olga paused before giving up her weapon.

Gracie took them all in with a dip of her head. She moved along to the next cupboard and opened it.

"What are they?" Artan said.

"Guns. Like the ones hanging from the bottoms of the drones."

Her arms folded across her chest, Olga sneered. "They don't look like the ones on the bottoms of the drones."

"They're not, really, but they do the same thing. They fire bullets."

"So," William said, "you have guns here, but we go outside carrying spears and swords?"

"We don't have a huge supply of bullets. Like the explosives along the hall, these guns are only for emergencies."

"Where do you get more bullets from?" Artan said.

"Aus—"

Whoosh!

As if he'd heard his name, Aus ran into the room like an enraged bull. Over six feet four inches, he had wide shoulders and thick arms. He charged over to one monitor. A crew of about ten men followed him in and gathered around him. While shaking his head, the glow from the monitors lighting up his puce skin, he said, "He'd best not give us away."

Gracie stepped closer, and Artan followed her. One of Aus' men stepped aside to give them a better view. Despite the energy Aus had brought into the room, the man smiled, and Artan smiled back. "Thank you."

"What's going on, Aus?" Gracie said.

"What does it fucking look like?"

"It looks like an empty screen, which is why I'm asking."

"We lost Trevor."

"Lost him?"

The young soldier with Aus, the one who'd given Artan space, couldn't have been any older than sixteen. Yet he had a confidence beyond his years. A confidence to speak when many others would have held their tongue. "He got separated from us when we were out on a raid. We were chased. We had to leave him behind."

"And is he—"

"There!" Aus pointed at the screen, cutting off Gracie's question.

Whoosh!

Jan entered the room. An older version of Aus. Slightly

taller. Slightly fatter. Slightly greyer. "Aus, what's going on? I heard you came back in a hurry."

Where he'd been hostile towards Gracie, Aus' tone softened at his dad's question. He pointed at the screen again. "Trevor got separated from us while we were out on a mission. We were chased."

"Are they still following him?" Jan said.

Aus shook his head. "I don't know." Trevor stood in shot on the screen and waited. He looked behind before staring at the camera.

"You'd best not blow our cover," Aus said. "I swear—"

"Why aren't you trying to help him?" William said.

Aus spun in William's direction. His shoulders hunched, and the whites of his eyes shone. Before he could speak, the boy who'd let Artan see the screen cut him off. "We have to be certain he's not being followed. Until we're sure it's safe, he's on his own. Whatever happens, we can't reveal this community. Too many people's lives depend on it." The boy turned to Artan with a tight-lipped smile. "It's the way. It's for the greater good."

Trevor took off and vanished from the screen. Seconds later, he stumbled back into shot. Blood ran down his face from a gash on his forehead. Several people came into view and set upon him, knocking him down and laying into him with punches and kicks.

"Fuck it!" Aus leaned over the console in front of the monitor and sighed. He shook his head and turned away from the screen as the people weighed in on Trevor, beating him limp. They continued to attack him until one of them stumbled into shot with a large rock raised above him. He dropped it on Trevor's head.

Artan's stomach tensed when Trevor's legs snapped rigid before falling limp.

"That …" Aus said, his thick index finger on his right

hand pointing at the screen, "is why we had to leave him. We can't risk showing them where we live. There are too many of them, and they're too dangerous."

"They're the same people we saw with the dogs," Gracie said.

Aus spun on his sister. His already flushed face turned a deep crimson. A vein lifted along his right temple. "You ran into them earlier?"

"No." Gracie lifted her chest and stepped closer to her brother. She spat when she spoke, her teeth clenched. "We *saw* them. We avoided them."

"Why do they hate you so much?" William said.

"They'll hate you the same as us." Aus pointed at William. "We all speak the same language. A different language to them. That's enough."

"Surely there's more to it than that?" William said.

"Well, look at you." Aus rolled his eyes. "You've been here five minutes and you think you can solve problems that have stumped us for decades." He closed the distance between him and William, shoving Artan aside on his way past. "Shall I say it slower for you? We. Don't. Speak. The. Same. Language. So whatever the reason for their hatred, we won't ever be able to understand it."

William's lips tightened, and he raised his chin. He breathed through his nose.

The boy who'd moved aside for Artan and Gracie rested his hand on Aus' shoulder and pulled him back from William. "You've made your point."

Something about the boy. The softness of his tone. The generosity of his compassion. It took the tension from Aus' tight frame. The large man nodded. "You're right. The fact is, we need someone to fill Trevor's place. We need another man."

"Or woman." Olga stepped forwards, her hands on her hips.

Aus looked her up and down and snorted a laugh. He turned his back on Olga. "If you all plan on staying here, we're going to take you out for a run with us in the hope one of you losers has something to offer. There are three fundamental rules when running with us." He used the fingers on his right hand to count them. "One, you don't get caught or seen. Two, if you get caught or seen, you don't come back here. Three, if you come back here because you thought you were safe, you wait long enough to be sure. If you've been followed, you make sure you don't give this community away. Don't look at the cameras. Don't go anywhere near one of the access hatches. Those fuckers up there outnumber us fifty to one. They find out where we are, and they'll take us down in a day. Do any of you think you have that in you?"

William shook his head. He'd already made it abundantly clear he wanted to leave as soon as possible, and after his brief interaction with Aus, there seemed little chance that the pair would work well together. Matilda also wanted to leave as soon as she could. Artan would go when they left, but what about Max? They needed him, and until he'd had time to rest, they were stuck here.

In the absence of an answer, Gracie said, "They sound like harsh rules, but we do what we can to keep this place safe. They're harsh, but necessary."

"We don't know how long we'll be here for," William said. "We'll be moving on as soon as we can."

"That depends on Max though, right?" Artan said. The attention of the room turned on him. His cheeks flushed. He coughed to clear his throat and said to Olga, "Right?"

She nodded. "Yeah. Speaking of which, I think we should see how he's doing."

Aus and his team stepped aside to let them leave the

room. Artan walked at the back, his face still hot under the scrutiny of the small army. The boy who'd allowed him access to the monitor patted him on the back and spoke so only Artan heard. "It all seems a bit much at first, but you get used to it."

Artan smiled back at the boy and followed the others out into the corridor. It had been a long day, but maybe he would get used to it. It had been a long time since he'd had the luxury of getting used to anything.

CHAPTER 4

"What a prick!" William threw his right hand up. "I mean, where does he get off by speaking to me like that? We want to help. We're on the same fucking side. Prick!"

William's echo agreed, bouncing off the hallway's hard steel walls. The dull lighting reminded him of the time. It urged him to keep the noise down so he didn't wake everyone. A sharp pain ran through his tight chest. His mind raced. He needed to centre himself. Whatever their next step, he couldn't formulate a plan in this state. He flinched when Matilda slipped her hand into his. But he held on, and they locked fingers, the warmth of her touch spreading through his tense upper body.

Their steps locked in stride, and the rest of them kept their noise down. Artan, Hawk, Olga, and Matilda all walked with William. Max had stayed back in their room, and Dianna had done nothing but sleep since they'd arrived in Dout.

Quieter this time, William said, "We need to get out of

this place as soon as possible. Either that, or I'm going to take a swing for that prick."

Matilda squeezed his hand again. She flashed him a tight-lipped smile. She had his back and would leave whenever he wanted, but he needed to calm down.

"I get that we're safer down here, although Aus seems like a liability, so I'm not sure *how* safe, but living underground is going to get old fast, right?"

Another tight-lipped smile from Matilda. The others stared ahead, their silence highlighted by the gentle whir of the ventilation fans. "Right?"

"Look, William—" Hawk avoided his eye and spoke in a whisper "—we're all tired."

"So tired you'd put up with that arsehole?"

Hawk shrugged. "I need a rest. We have beds here. Food. Shelter. This has to be one of the safest options right now. Surely you must be feeling the strain from the life we've been living?"

Every one of William's muscles buzzed with fatigue. Each step threw down the challenge to his body: see if it could remain standing for this one. He'd been able to push through it so far, but Hawk had a point. Where would they find a better place to rest?

"Also," Hawk said, "we decide as a group, and I can't speak for Dianna—"

"Where is she?" Olga said.

"Resting. Like Max."

"Not like Max." A shake of her head, Olga's familiar sneer returned, twisting her features. "She's not done a fraction of what Max has for our group."

"Whatever." Hawk rolled his eyes. "She's resting."

William's pounding heart beat harder. He fought to keep his tone even. "And how long do you think she'll need? We can't wait forever."

Hawk shrugged and scratched his scarred neck. "I can't speak for her."

"You know," Artan said, "I could do with some time to get my strength up too."

William let go of his tension with a sigh.

"I'm sorry, man," Artan said.

Matilda squeezed William's hand again.

"It is what it is," William said. "This isn't a dictatorship. We go with the majority."

"Getting past that wall won't be easy," Hawk said.

Olga this time, "And I'm guessing we'll need Max on top form."

The entrance to their dorm looked like many other doors in the long hallway. Just the sight of it turned William's legs bandy. He needed to rest. They all did. "I suppose we need to see how he's doing. Without him on board, we have no plan." He slapped his palm against the button. *Crack!*

The door slid aside with a *whoosh!*

"Get the fuck away from me." A butter knife in one hand and a fork in the other, Max stood in the room completely naked. The whites of his eyes shone in the gloom. His lips peeled back to reveal his gritted teeth. "I will use these."

"Max." Olga stepped forwards with her hands raised. "It's us. You don't need to worry."

William led the others in. They fanned out, surrounding Max.

A slash of his butter knife, Max shook with the force of his words. "Stay the fuck back. I didn't mean to kill those kids." He knocked against his own head with his knuckles. "But they were closing in on me. They wouldn't give me any space." He knocked several times as if sounding out the syllables against his skull. "Why didn't they just leave me alone? I didn't want to hurt them."

William raised his eyebrows at Matilda before returning to Max.

Crying from unblinking eyes, Max shook his head. "They wouldn't leave me alone. What else could I d—oomph!"

Olga tackled Max, slamming her shoulder into his stomach and sending them both onto Max's bed.

Artan and Hawk pinned him down. Each of them tried to prize the cutlery from his clenched fists. William and Matilda went for his legs.

Snarling like a diseased, Max bucked and flipped. A man possessed.

Like trying to throw a hat on the head of a wild bull, Olga tried to cover his dignity with the bedsheets, but they fell from his twisting form.

Max snarled and hissed. His voice strained, he said, "They were getting too close to me. I didn't want to kill kids, but the diseased were closing in. They called me Mad Max. They had bleeding eyes. I didn—"

Crack! Artan caught Max with a clean shot to the chin, silencing him and turning him instantly limp. Sweat glistened on his brow as he pulled Max's fingers free from the knife's handle and threw it across the room. It clattered on the steel floor and crashed into the wall. Panting, he wiped his face, stepped away from the flaccid and naked Max, and said, "I'm sorry, Olga."

"It's fine." She shrugged. "Were it anyone else, I would have done the same."

"What on earth was he talking about?" William stepped away from the bed while Olga covered Max again.

"I don't know." Olga stroked Max's head. The weak light in the room caught the tears in her eyes. "Whatever it is, I'm sorry to say this, William, but he needs more time."

And how could William argue with that? "I know. And it doesn't matter what any of us want to hear, we need to do what's right for the group. Me having to deal with Aus being an arsehole is nothing compared to what's going on inside that poor bastard's head."

"I think we should take it in turns watching him," Olga said. "Just in case he wakes up in the same state."

William nodded his agreement with the others.

"I'll take the first shift." Olga sat down on the bed beside Max and stroked his hair away from his face while letting go of a hard sigh.

Their dorm had one circular communal room and separate pods leading from it. At some point, especially if they stayed a while, they would use the private rooms. But not tonight. Tonight, they needed to support Olga and watch over Max.

"Where's Dianna?" Artan said.

Hawk looked at one of the doors leading to the separate pods. "She's sleeping in one of the rooms on her own."

Artan sat on his bed, slipped off his trousers, and slid beneath the covers. "That's good. At least it kept her away from Max in that state."

Matilda sat beside William and put an arm around him. She kissed the side of his face, her warm breath against his skin when she spoke in a whisper. "We will get out of here; we just need to be patient. We all need a bit of time."

"Yeah." William nodded and kissed her back. "Max has just shown me I can cope with Aus. No matter how much I hate him, it's nothing compared to what he's dealing with right now."

Matilda smiled. "And if he turns into too much of a liability, we'll kick his arse." She kissed him again. "Night, William. Love you." She walked over to her bed.

William smiled, but his heart remained heavy. How much longer would they have to spend in this place? He lay on his bed, his body thrumming with fatigue. The low light turned the others into silhouettes. Artan and Hawk were now lumps beneath their covers. Matilda twisted and turned to get comfortable. Max was out cold. Olga silently sobbed, her shoulders shaking with her muted grief. How long would it be before Max got his head together? They needed him. How else would they get past the wall? But how much of the old Max would return? Would they ever see the kid they'd spent national service with? And what if, no matter how long they waited, he was never ready to leave?

CHAPTER 5

Clack!
     The teeth snapped so close to Max the sound went through him like it came from his own breaking spine.
Clack!
He shoved the creature away, and it stumbled into the wall of diseased two feet behind it. Its jaw mashed with a palsied gurn. It lurched forward and grabbed him. He held it back, his arms shaking. It bit at the air between them.
Clack! Clack! Clack!
Max shoved, but the creature held on. "Get off me! Get the fuck off me!"
A hard kick broke their connection and forced the diseased back. The others closed in with pawing hands. They grabbed him all over his body. The more he twisted and fought, the tighter they clung on, their clasp stinging and bruising his skin.
Thud!
Max woke when he hit the cold steel floor. He kicked the covers away and jumped up, fists raised. Soaked in sweat. Panting. Alone in their communal room. He sat on

the edge of his bed. Where had the others gone? He dragged his sheets from the floor and pulled them around himself. They both dried and warmed his rapidly cooling body. He opened and closed his aching jaw, testing the bruise with the tips of his fingers. How long had he been out? What about the kids in the canteen? If anything bad had happened, surely someone would have come for him by now.

Whoosh!

The door to the dorm opened. The tock of his friends' steps entered. Each one of their purposeful strides snapped through him. *Clack! Clack! Clack!*

Olga led the line. She walked towards him, carrying a plate with a small bread roll and a lump of cheese. "I've brought you some food, seeing as you've not had breakfast, lunch, or dinner today."

Max's stomach bucked. He shook his head while raising a halting hand at her. "Thank you, but I'll give it a miss."

"You need to eat *something*."

"And soon," Hawk said. "We're wanted in the sports hall."

"What?" Max's heart rate quickened.

Artan sat on his bed and switched tops to a cleaner one. Lithe and muscly. The frame of a boy, but he fought like a man. "Aus wants to see us all in the sports hall."

No. He needed more time. "You go without me."

A warm hand against his cold skin, Olga smiled. "It'll be okay, sweet. We're with you."

It won't fucking be okay. But how could he get out of it?

"How are you feeling now?" William said.

"What do you mean?"

"From last night. When—"

A glance from Olga cut him off.

What happened last night? "The kids?"

"Huh?" William said.

"It doesn't matter." Olga threw some clothes down beside Max. "Just get changed. Come on."

~

Every sound cut to Max's core as if someone had raised the world's volume and then funnelled it directly into his being. His friends' steps against the steel floor. The whoosh of doors opening in the distance. The occasional laugh, cut-off conversations, a child crying … They all pierced his outer layer and drove probing needles into his soft self.

Max snapped his hand away when Olga tried to hold it.

Although she smiled at him, it stood in stark contrast to her furrowed brow.

"I'm sorry." He reached out to her, their fingers interlocking.

William led the line, turning down one of the main corridors towards the pleasure dome.

"I'm sorry," Max said again. "I'm a little sensitive to stimulation right now."

Another smile. Another confused frown. Olga nodded. "It's fine. Take your time. Things will get better."

Will they?

Whoosh!

Max had spent most of his time in their room, so he let the others guide him and walked at the back of the line. The echo of his friends' steps changed as they entered the tunnel. It led to an open arena. The sports hall. He turned full circle. Hard to tell how many people it would take to fill the surrounding seats. Enough to make him feel tiny by comparison. Not quite the ice hockey rink they'd been taken to by Fear's army, but the red-uniformed soldier still flew through his mind's eye. She got launched from the plank into the crowd of diseased all over again. Her bleeding stare. Her snapp—

The touch of Olga's hand against his pulled Max back into the room with a gasp. She leaned close enough for her breath to tickle his ear. Too close. "I'm right beside you."

How could he tell her he didn't want anyone there? If only he could be on his own.

Aus, Gracie's older brother, lined them up side by side. They occupied a small space on the wooden-floored court. It stretched about one hundred feet long by about fifty feet wide. Gracie stood nearby with a group of eight boys and young men. His friends were at ease with the small army. Like they already knew them.

His hands behind his back, Aus paced up and down in front of them. Every step hit the wooden floor with a *crack* and ran to the high ceiling, whipping around the cavernous space. "We're going out on a mission tonight."

A diseased scream tore through Max's mind. He gasped, closed his eyes, and balled his fists.

Aus' steps halted.

Max opened his eyes again.

Tilting his large head to one side, Aus sneered. "Gasp all you want, sunshine. What I can promise you is there ain't no free rides in this place."

"Just carry on with what you were saying," Olga said.

"I'll speak when I'm ready."

"Well, be ready, then."

Aus held Olga's glare for several seconds. His already puce face moved to a deeper shade of crimson. He resumed his march up and down in front of the group. "You don't get to stay here for free. And you all saw what happened to Trevor yesterday."

Max raised his eyebrows at Olga, who shook her head. He didn't need to worry about it now.

"We need someone to replace him," Aus continued. He paused in front of Dianna and looked her up and down before smirking again. Clearly not her, then. Although, where had she come from? She hadn't walked over with them.

"What if we don't want to be a part of your crew?" William stepped forward from the line. "We've done nothing but spend time outside amongst the diseased; what makes you think we want to go out there again? Especially if you expect us to take orders while we're there."

Crack! Crack! Crack! The closer Aus walked to William, the harder his steps. He paused in front of him. Only an inch between their noses. Were Max in William's shoes, he would have shoved Aus back. "I don't give a fuck what you've done. What, you want me to compensate you for the hard life you've had?" His bottom lip turned down, and he spoke with a mocking baby tone. "Poor wittle William. He's had a hard life and wants time to rest."

Aus' face changed, and he shouted, spraying William with spittle. "In case you've not noticed, you prick, we've all had a fucking hard life! Now grow the fuck up!"

William rested his forehead against Aus'. Faced with Gracie's brother's rage, he spoke in a soft tone. "I'll tell you what, Aus. You get off your power trip, and we'll come outside with you. How does that sound?"

Aus stepped back from William and raised his right fist so it hovered beside his face.

Clunk!

The lights went off. The darkness closed in around Max. It pushed against him.

Olga grabbed his hand.

Thunk! A brilliant white light from the back row of the seating area shone on William. It sent him stumbling back a few paces. It threw a long shadow out behind him and hid Aus, Gracie, and the rest of Aus' crew in the darkness.

A voice in the shadows, Aus said, "You say whatever you need to say to appease your ego, William. The fact remains; you want to stay in this community, you need to pull your weight, which means coming out with us tonight. And after this trial, we're going to pick one of you to run with us while you're here. We're a man down; we need to fill that spot."

It stung Max's eyes to watch William squint from the light's glare.

Clack!

Clack!

Clack!

Aus resumed his pacing in front of Max and his friends. He walked to one end of the line towards Dianna before turning around and closing in on Max at the other end.

Another cold sweat turned Max's body damp. The salty secretion burned his already sore eyes. He needed to sleep for days to feel somewhere even close to himself again.

Clack!

Clack!

Clack!

Aus halted in front of Max. "You okay there, son?"

The light shifted from William to Max. He raised his hands to shield his eyes.

"I'm talking to you," Aus said.

The light turned off and threw them back into complete darkness. Max's heart beat harder. The predatory shadows closed in again. A snarl in the corner of the room. A diseased. They'd brought a fucking diseased in here.

"Well!" Aus said.

Clack! Snapping jaws. The groans of discontent. Yelps of discomfort from playing host to the vile disease.

Thunk! The lights came on again. Aus stood an inch from Max and smothered him with his hot breath. It smelled like biscuits. His yell reverberated through Max's skull. "I said *well?*"

Aus' words trailed off and morphed into snarls. Growls. Moans. Crimson spread across his eyes. A screen of blood. His mouth stretched wide.

"No," Max said.

Aus stepped back. "Are you slow or something? Are you struggling to keep up? I'm telling you what's happening. We're going outside tonight."

Max stepped forwards and shook his head. "No."

The same sneer he'd worn since Max and his friends entered, Aus threw his head back with a laugh. "I'll say it again; you're coming outside."

"I think you're the one who's slow, so I'll say it again to see if we can get that brain cell working in your head. No. I'm. Not."

"You'll do what I say!" Aus' face slipped. The disease took command of his features. He lunged forward.

Max met his charge and tackled him to the ground. He climbed on top of him and grabbed his lapels. His rage tore at his throat as if his words were shards of broken glass. "I'm not going outside. No matter what you say. You can't fucking make me."

Aus' response morphed into snarls and yowls. He bit at the air between them. A cut opened up on his face. He turned into the eight-year-old boy from the dining hall.

"I didn't do anything to those kids. That wasn't me." Max lifted Aus' torso and slammed it back down again. "I didn't do it." And again. "I didn't do it."

Hands grabbed Max and dragged him away. A diseased came around in front of him. No, not a diseased.

"Max!" Olga said. Clearly not the first time she'd said it.

"You're mental!" Back on his feet, Aus pointed at Max and then at his own temple. "You're mad in the head."

Max stood at ease, and his friends let him go. He stepped towards Aus. At first, Olga shoved him back, but he nodded at her. He had this. The room had fallen silent, Max's steps the only sound in the large hall. He smiled. It turned into a tittering laugh.

Aus' face turned pale.

"You know what, you're right." Max laughed again and shook his head. Tears of mirth blurred his vision. "We need to help. I can go outside. I can do this." He tugged on Aus' arm. "Come on, let's go. I'm up for this." He howled, his wild call filling the vast arena. "I'm ready to go to war."

The attention of the room shifted from Max to Aus, who opened and closed his mouth several times.

"Come on," Max said. "Let's not fuck about. Let's get this show on the road."

Aus shook his head and backed towards the tunnel leading out of there. The shadows from the tight walkway swamped him. "You're a fucking liability. Olga, take him back to your dorm and then come and find us. That lunatic will get us all killed if we take him outside."

The others passed Max. They followed Aus out. None of them looked back at him.

Just Olga and Max remained. She shrugged. "What on earth was that about?"

Max laughed. "What?"

Olga shook her head and led him out of the room.

In the hallway, the distant sound of crashing pans from the kitchen. His and Olga's steps. A door opened somewhere. A baby cried.

Whoosh! Olga moved aside to let Max into their room first.

"So what are we doing here?" Max laughed again.

"Sit down!" Olga pointed at the bed.

"Huh?"

She raised her voice. "Sit the fuck down. Now."

Max sat on his bed.

"I don't know what that was about. I know you've been through a lot of shit."

"You have no fucking idea," Max said. His smile fell.

"Maybe you're right, but what I know is you're going to get us all killed if you don't get your shit together. I don't know why you just did what you did, but you've made us a target. *All* of us."

"I—"

"Shut up, Max! Now, we're going out tonight with Aus and his crew. Hopefully, we'll all be coming back. Next time you want to put on a performance like that … don't, okay?"

Max sniffed against his running nose. He touched his damp cheeks. He'd been crying. The lump in his throat cut off his response.

As Olga left the room, she said, "Whatever you need to do to get your head straight, do it."

Whoosh! The doors closed behind her and muted her steps until they faded away.

Max fell back onto his bed. He lay in his dorm alone. His only company came from the echo of his own sobs. Every time he blinked, the crimson glare from the diseased punched through his mind. Their tortured snarls and yowls echoed through his skull.

Clack!

Their teeth snapped at him.

Clack!

He clamped his hands to the sides of his head, trying to shut them out.

Clack!

CHAPTER 6

Thud! Thud! Thud! Artan turned to Olga, who ran along the corridor towards them.

Since leaving the sports hall, Aus had led them in silence. He'd taken them to the surveillance room, where they picked up weapons. Artan took several spears, a sheath to carry them on his back, and a knife. He handed Olga the sword he'd taken for her. She took it with a nod, her sweating face glistening in the tunnel's dulled light. She acknowledged the rest of their crew. William, Matilda, Hawk, Dianna, and even Gracie.

Aus halted, but maintained the silence. Artan shifted his weight from one foot to the other. He looked at Nick, who raised his eyebrows back at him. They needed to be patient. Let Aus do his thing.

Twice her height and three times her weight, Aus approached Olga, rested his hands on his hips, and leaned over her.

Were Artan a betting man, he still would have backed Olga. She might have been small, but so were coiled springs.

She ground her jaw, unflinching while she returned Aus' glare.

"You seem to be the only one that boy listens to. You need to make sure he winds his neck in fast. Your time here will be short if he doesn't."

The delivery might have been rough, but Aus had a point. And Olga clearly agreed. Her jaw jutting out, she acquiesced with the slightest inclination of her head.

"He's been through a lot," Gracie said. "Were it not for him, I wouldn't have made it back here alive."

Aus' snorted a humourless laugh. "That's even more of a reason for us to kick him out."

Several of his crew sniggered. Nick didn't.

"Fuck you, Aus, you prick. Why don't you shelve all this alpha-male bullshit? I know it makes you and your band of boys hard, but it gets in the way of you doing a half-decent job. Now, are we going out tonight or what?"

The sniggering boys bristled and watched Aus like obedient dogs awaiting their owner's instructions.

"You know the rules," Aus said. He walked to the end of the tunnel and the ladder rungs embedded in the wall. Their exit, a hatch in the ceiling about thirty feet above. "But I'll say them again. One: Don't get caught or seen. Two: If you get caught or seen, don't come back here. Three: If you come back here and someone's following you, don't try to get in or wave at the cameras. Don't let this entire community fall because you fucked up. Trevor didn't, and I gave much more of a shit about Trevor than I do about any of you lot. Four: Follow what we do, and at the end of this, we'll pick one of you to run with us."

William shook his head to himself.

Aus reached up and grabbed a rung. "Our anonymity is our greatest strength. Any of you lot come even close to jeopardising that, and I will personally cut your throats. That includes you, Gracie."

"You've been looking for an excuse to do that since we were kids."

The hatch at the top of the ladder clicked when Aus pushed it open. A steel sheet several feet above it kept them covered. Rain hammered against it. One of Aus' crew shook his head. "I hate rain."

Aus slid the steel sheet aside. It let in a cool breeze that rushed down to meet them at the bottom of the ladder. Spots of rain landed cold drops on Artan's face.

The top half of Aus vanished from sight, and he paused. Clearly satisfied with what he saw, or what he didn't see, he climbed out of the hatch, his team following him one after the other.

～

THE RAIN FELL in sheets and stung the top of Artan's head. Aus' crew stood shoulder to shoulder, a few feet from the hatch, their backs turned on him and his friends. He walked around the side and halted next to Nick. "Shit!"

Nick's eyes were glazed. His mouth hung loose. Artan touched his arm and mouthed, *You okay?*

Stupid fucking question. Ask it to the wrong person and he'd be sure to get a mouthful of abuse. But Nick clearly got the sentiment and nodded.

The loud rain muffled Artan's words. Hopefully, only Nick heard him. "Trevor?"

Nick's lips tightened, and he dipped a nod.

"Shit!" Gracie shoved through Aus' line of men and walked towards Trevor. Someone had strung him up, much like the man they'd found in the ruined city. The one who'd been eaten alive by the scavengers. Except, instead of hanging suspended like a star, his arms had been stretched out to his sides and his legs were bound at his ankles. They'd attached him to the wall of a ruined building. "We need to cut him down."

Aus grabbed the back of Gracie's collar and dragged her away. His bared teeth shone in the darkness. "This is why you should remain inside. We cut him down and they'll know we've been here. After they've worked that out—" he pointed to where they'd all emerged from "—how long will it take for them to find that entrance?" The lights from Dout shone from the still-open hatch.

As the last to climb out, William closed the hatch and slid the sheet of steel back into place.

Holding William with a lingering stare, his eyes tight, Aus dared him to react.

William's eyes deadened, and he maintained eye contact. Obviously Artan had his back, but if he had a choice, he'd rather not fight those giving them shelter.

"Come on," Aus said, "let's go." He led them off at a jog, his crew behind him. His crew and Hawk, who elbowed his way to the front of the pack.

The rain came down harder than before. Hawk shouted over it, "Aus, if you're looking for someone to run with you, I don't mind being that person while we're here. I used to lead the hunts in the last place I lived."

"What were you hunting?" Aus said. "Rocks? With a voice as loud as yours, I'm surprised you caught anything other than a cold."

Artan clearly had competition for the place on Aus' team. He raised his eyebrows at Nick. The boy pressed down on the air with his hands as if to encourage patience from him. *It'll be fine. Just wait.*

"Sorry," Hawk said, "I just wanted to—"

Aus halted, spun to the left, shoved Hawk aside, and

threw his spear. His group raised their weapons as one. A well-drilled team, they loosed their spears one after the other. They ended the diseased charge before it began. The creatures fell with weak gargles.

Artan hunched beneath the rain's onslaught. When Nick straightened his back, he spoke in a whisper. "How did you see them?"

"We heard them," Nick said.

The rain slammed against the cracked road, a continuous wash around them. "I'm struggling to even hear you right now."

Nick smiled. "It takes practice. You'll learn to hear past the rain." He took off with the rest of Aus' crew. They ran in the direction they'd launched their spears. A minute later, every one of them had retrieved their weapons.

∽

Artan still climbed the hill when Aus reached the top and pulled a pair of binoculars from his pocket. His crew joined him one by one and scanned their surroundings, Hawk among them.

His legs aching from the climb, Artan joined the others and caught his breath. They overlooked a community surrounded by a wall. Much like Edin's, they'd made it from rocks, but it only stood about ten feet tall and two to three feet thick. Easy enough to climb, but sufficient for protecting against the diseased.

Aus pressed a thick finger to his lips. More for Artan and his friends than the others. He pointed at the community below, gave his team a thumbs up, and took off again. They all followed, this time in single file.

Hawk cut in front of Artan, so he ran directly behind Aus' team. But being farther back gave Artan time to see what lay ahead. He slipped his spear into the harness on his back while tracking Aus' progress. Something he could hopefully replicate. The thick-set man moved with a grace that didn't suit his stature. He leaped at the wall, gripped the wet rock with his thick hands, moved up it like a lizard, and vaulted over the top. It took him about three seconds from start to finish.

The rough rocks stung Artan's hands when he began his climb. All of Aus' crew had vanished over the top by the time he'd reached halfway. But better to take his time than hurt himself. The light from the moon turned the wall into a glistening craggy surface of foot- and handholds. Each time he shoved his toe onto a ledge or gripped on, he tested it would hold his weight before he climbed to the next point.

The top of the rough wall grazed Artan's stomach when he lay across it and threw himself over. He bent his legs to absorb the shock of his landing on the other side, his feet squelching in the damp ground.

Nick offered him his hand to help him stand straight. He held on longer than necessary. "You okay?"

Artan half-smiled. "So far."

Hawk landed next, hitting the ground like a falling rock. Gracie. Matilda. Olga, and then William followed.

"Where's Dianna?" Artan said.

Olga rolled her eyes. "She didn't even try to climb the wall. I think she was worried she might break a nail." She shrugged. "I think she said something about helping the community in other ways. To be honest, I stopped listening."

"Shh!" Aus pressed his fingers to his lips.

The outside of this community might have had a wall like Edin's, and the houses on the inside were roughly the same height, but the similarities ended there. People with more advanced techniques built these houses. Straight brick walls, pitched roofs, glass windows. Most of them glowed from lights on the inside. The steady illumination of electricity.

Aus led them on again. They weaved through the houses, sticking to the paths. The rain continued lashing down. Artan's soaked clothes clung to him.

They passed a building with one of its windows opened a crack. Cooked meat and spices fragranced the air. Artan's mouth watered. It would almost be worth getting caught to try some. The chatter of people inside put him off. They spoke in a language he didn't recognise.

A dog growled and yelped in the distance. Several more took up the call. Artan's pulse sped. Did they know there were intruders in their community? And if they set the animals loose, how would they outrun a pack of hounds?

Aus reached the end of another small house and halted, pushing the others against the wall behind him with a sweep of his arm. The brickwork rough against his soaked back, Artan focused on regulating his breathing while he waited.

Several people walked past where they'd nearly gone. Another danger Artan hadn't heard. Why would Aus and his crew want him to run with them when he had such dulled senses?

His index finger and thumb of his right hand pressed together to form a ring that gestured they were okay, Aus led them on.

The silhouette of a massive building loomed ahead. They ran into its deep shadows cast by the moonlight. There were no paths close to the building, the ground boggy, their steps squelching. Artan and his friends' steps were the loudest of them all.

Artan leaned against the huge building, pulling in next to the tall and slim Nick. Hawk had overtaken even him in his quest to be closer to Aus. Where William had taken up the rear, Gracie now took his place. It made sense to have someone with a bit more experience watching their backs.

They made slow progress, walking on tiptoes around the side of the enormous building. A sea of solar panels stretched away from them. They covered an area of at least three thousand square feet. The glow from the moon revealed the farmland beyond. Were it not for the rain hitting the panels, this place would have been the quietest spot in the entire community. With nothing but solar panels and farmland, what reasons were there to visit here in the dark?

With fewer buildings for shelter, the wind cut into Artan's sodden form.

Aus broke from the side of the building and led them to the solar panels. A screwdriver in his hand, he dropped and went to work while his men arrived and lined up. One after the other, they took a liberated section, each piece about a foot square.

Hawk took a panel and waited for another.

"That's enough," Aus said. "Believe me, if you're running for your life, you want to make sure you can carry what you have; otherwise, why take it?"

Hawk turned away, and Nick took the next panel, Artan the one after that. Heavy like a large ceramic tile, he reached his left arm over it and held it to his body. He could still grab a spear if he needed. He returned to the shadows alongside the barn.

"Why doesn't the power go out?" Artan said.

Nick leaned close and kept his voice low. "The solar panels charge the batteries that power the community. As long as the batteries stay connected to their mains, they'll be none the wiser until morning."

"And you do this often?"

"When it's necessary, but not so often they feel the need to put guards out here. They can make more panels. There's another community, which you will see at some point. I think they must assume they're the ones robbing them, and for a few solar panels, it's not worth going to war."

"So if they have the tech to make solar panels, surely they can live with more luxuries than the ones they have?"

"They have heat, power, and food." Nick shrugged. "You've seen where they came from, right?"

"Not really." Artan shook his head. "We saw them come through the gates in the wall, but we don't know what's on the other side."

"True, but it's enough to know they're the enemy of whoever lives there."

"Are we their enemy too?"

"They don't send people through who speak our language, so it's led us to assume we're not. But, as for the people in this community, they were sent through the gates with one purpose."

"To be turned into diseased?" Artan said.

"Exactly. So they need to live under the radar. Create a community that's too large and they'll show they're still alive. No matter how well equipped, or how advanced their tech, I'm guessing it pales in comparison to an army led by the people who built the wall."

As the last in line, Gracie took the final solar panel tile before Aus removed one for himself. He overtook those waiting for him and led them back the way they'd come from. At least, it had started out as them retreading their path, but he changed their route. They had a clear run to the wall, yet he took them deeper into the maze of walkways running through the buildings. He brought them to a halt by a house and handed his solar tile to one of his crew. Freeing a knife from a sheath at his hip, he had the screwdriver he'd used on the panels in his other hand, which he used to pry open the house's window. He bit his bottom lip, the window's hinges groaning when he pulled it open, and climbed inside.

Too far back to see into the house, Artan winced when someone grunted. He twisted where he stood at the wet squelches of repeated stabbings. And then silence.

A panting Aus climbed back out again. His knife and hand glistened with fresh blood. Wild eyes. Bared teeth. He hissed. "An eye for an eye—"

"Turns the whole world blind." Gracie scowled at her brother.

Despite keeping his voice at only a whisper, the weight of Aus' growl shook as if it came from the heavens. "What the fuck do you know? That was for Trevor."

"No." Gracie shook her head. "That was for you. Trevor's dead. Getting revenge won't change that."

Freddie, a short and stocky man with dark skin and a mohawk, tugged on Aus' arm. "Come on, we can't hang around here arguing."

Just before they set off again, Artan leaned close to Nick. "Does he always do shit like that?"

"Only when he feels like a score needs to be settled." Nick ran off next, and Artan followed.

∽

S*QUELCH*! Artan landed next to Nick and cleared the way to let Olga drop behind him.

Dianna, who sat on a nearby grassy bank, stood up at their approach. Hawk threw his arms out to the sides and glanced at Aus before he said, "What was that about?"

"What?" Dianna said.

"We were *all* supposed to go on that run. What gives you the right to bottle it?"

"Fuck off, Hawk. The fact you were with them is what made me hold back."

"What?"

"We nearly died in the ruined city because you're a weapons-grade liability who wanted to fight every diseased in the place." She pointed at the community. "You think I want to follow someone like you in there?"

The rain continued to assault the top of Artan's head, every drop a nail hammered into his skull. But he still caught the slightest growl riding the wind. The clumsy steps. The phlegmy snarl from where the creature struggled for breath.

Hawk and Dianna continued arguing while the diseased headed straight for them. Had no one else heard it? If Artan took it down now, Hawk wouldn't forgive him. How would Aus accept him onto his team if he couldn't hear the threat to his own life?

But Hawk clearly hadn't heard it. And the diseased presented a threat not only to his own life, but to Dianna's too.

The creature's breathing grew heavier. The squelching steps closer. Artan's solar panel under his left arm, he pulled his spear free with his right. Just in case.

The moonlight shone on the creature now fifteen feet to Hawk and Dianna's left. Its long hair sodden. Its teeth bared. It charged. Artan launched his spear. It slammed into the side of the diseased's head. A bullseye into its right temple. It stumbled past Dianna and Hawk and fell limp on the ground just a few feet away.

Everyone fell silent. Their collective attention turned on Artan.

Hawk's chin wobbled, and his face flushed red. His jaw tightened. How fucking dare Artan show him up like that?

"If you're done with your little argument?" Aus said. "We'll be moving on. Are you done?"

A few seconds' pause, Hawk then dipped a sheepish nod.

Aus led the way. Nick patted Artan on the back as he passed him. "You're a fast learner."

Even after what had just happened, Hawk took up the same spot, directly behind Aus and his crew.

∼

Aus went last this time, sliding the steel sheet back across the gap and closing the hatch behind him as he climbed down the ladder. They'd left the hatch unlocked when they went out. He now secured it. *You come back with the crew, or they lock you out like they had with Trevor.*

Jumping from the last few rungs, Aus landed with a flat-footed *crack!* "That was the easier community of the two to rob."

Soaked and now surrounded by cold steel, Artan shivered and hugged himself for warmth.

Their illuminated surroundings picked out the traces of blood on Aus' hands and clothes. "Now we have to pick the person to run with us." He focused on Artan.

"Fuck this," Hawk said. He threw his weapons to the floor and walked off down the corridor.

"If you want it, that is?" Aus said.

Artan shrugged. "Yeah." He glanced at Nick before returning his attention to Aus. "For as long as we remain here."

They walked back in silence. Despite the distance separating them, a palpable tension hung between Artan and Hawk. Between William and Aus. Dianna and all of her old team. Gracie and her brother. In a sea of stoicism, Nick walked with the hint of a smile. The rest of the team didn't seem to give a shit about Artan, but at least he had one ally on Aus' crew.

Back at the armoury, Artan returned his spears to Aus, who said, "I'll see you next time we go out, then. And well done. I didn't think any of you lot had it in you, but you showed you might be an asset."

William, Matilda, and Olga had already followed Hawk out of there. Artan jogged to catch up with his friends and fell into stride behind them. He had a job for as long as they remained. Now they had to decide just how long they planned on staying.

CHAPTER 7

Crack! William hit the button to enter their dorm so hard it stung his palm. The automatic door slid aside, revealing their messy room in the dim light. None of them had made their beds. Were he on his own, he would have made it every day, but he didn't have it in him to fight a losing battle. Of all of them, Olga cared the least about order. They'd all lowered their standards rather than expected an elevation of hers. With so much else going on, a battle with Olga to be tidier sat very low on his list of priorities.

William entered the room first, Matilda behind him. Artan came in last. He slapped the button to close the door.

"We need a plan," William said. The blank faces around him forced him to elaborate. "We need to make a plan as to when we're going to leave this place. I can't stay here forever. Surely we can set a target and aim for it?"

"And you're still convinced it's a good idea?" Dianna said. "After what you've seen at the wall?"

William nodded. "Yeah, I do. We've come this far; why wouldn't we go all the way now?"

"Uh, I dunno. Maybe because they send scores of people

through the wall to die? I'm not convinced the paradise you're looking for is on the other side."

"I was talking to Nick while we were in that community tonight," Artan said, "and he said the people who come through the gates differ from us. They don't speak our language."

"Huh?" Dianna said.

William cut in, "It suggests that whoever's on the other side of the wall might be an ally. That what we're witnessing from this side is how they treat their enemies. And they might have good reason to send them here."

"And if they don't?"

"Look at what that community did to Trevor when they caught him," William said. "That suggests they're not good people. Besides, we'll never know unless we try to cross."

"I'm ready to leave when you are," Hawk said. He folded his arms across his chest, chewed his own tongue, and continued to stare at Artan.

"We need to give Max time," Artan said.

"Why did you throw that fucking spear?" Hawk threw his arms up.

Artan dragged a deep breath in through his nose.

William tensed, ready to step in.

"He saved your life," Matilda said.

Artan shrugged. "And Dianna's. That thing was about to take you both down."

"You should have let me fight my own battles," Hawk said.

Dianna rested her hand on Artan's forearm and glared at Hawk when she said, "I'm glad you did it. It's not the first time *he's* put us in danger."

"*What?*" Hawk shook his head, and his nostrils flared. He jabbed a thick finger in Dianna's direction. "Don't forget I went to the Asylum to bust you out."

"Don't forget I stopped you hanging yourself. I'd say that makes us even."

William stepped back as if struck by the savage comment. "Wow!" Matilda raised her eyebrows at him.

Hawk's jaw hung open, and he ran his fingers along the rope burns around his neck. He rubbed them, his eyes glazing as he stared into the middle distance.

But Dianna kept going, jabbing her finger in Hawk's direction. "You've been nothing but a liability since we left the asylum. It's like you've been trying to get us killed."

"I've been trying to make up for—"

"Selling your friends out to Magma and Ranger?" Dianna swiped a strand of hair behind her ear. "You really think it's that easy to make up for your betrayal? Were I them, I'd never forgive you. Especially when your attempts at making good will probably get everyone killed. You're a fucking liability."

Artan stepped between Hawk and Dianna. "William, I'll leave with you whenever you're ready to go. Until that moment, I'll run with Aus and his crew." He reached out to his sister and held her hand. "We won't get separated again."

Some of William's tension slid from his back. At least they had Artan on side.

"I don't enjoy staying here one bit," Hawk said. "How much longer do we have to wait, Olga?"

Deep bags sat beneath Olga's eyes. She arched an eyebrow. "Huh?"

"Max is your boyfriend. He's the reason we haven't already left."

"Steady on, Hawk," William said. "Maybe we should all have a rest and talk about it in the morning. We're all tired. We're all saying things we don't mean."

"I'm not," Dianna said.

"It's okay," Olga said. "Hawk, are you forgetting what Max

has done for us? What we needed him to do. Hell, what we *expected* him to do. We're the reason he's in this state. Also, we all know this isn't about Max. Were you good enough to be taken on by Aus, you'd no doubt be singing a very different tune."

"I stood more of a chance than you."

William flinched with every one of Olga's slow claps. The hard walls amplified each sharp crack. "Oh, well done," she said. "You're taking credit now because you have a penis."

Hawk balled his fists, and William edged closer to him. They were all under a lot of stress, but if he swung for Olga—

"Just tell us when Max will be ready to leave," Hawk said.

Olga's tone turned shrill. "How the hell would I—"

Whoosh!

Max appeared in the doorway leading to one of the private pods.

"Go on then," Olga said, turning her rage on Max.

William said, "Olga, d—"

"Shut the fuck up, William. Max, they all want to know when your head will be right again. We all want to leave and can't because of you."

Max's wild blue eyes flitted from one person to the next. Every time William saw him, his skin had turned another shade paler. His face gaunt, his cheeks sallow, his shoulders hunched. "I-I d-d-don't know." He shook his head and lost focus while staring at the floor. "I don't know. What do you mean? How can I—"

"Max"—William stepped towards their traumatised friend—"please don't worry. Everyone's tired and getting emotional. At some point we plan to leave, but we want to make sure you're okay before we do that." The words stuck in his throat. If he could leave now, he would, but they all needed to be ready. "Take your time. I'm sure you'll feel better soon."

Max scratched his head so hard William winced. He clawed at his scalp as if he could gouge out the crazy. "I'm a screw-up, aren't I?"

"Just use this time to get some rest," Matilda said.

Max rocked where he stood and shook his head. "I'm a screw-up. I'm keeping you all here. And now you're all arguing because of me."

"Because of Hawk," Dianna said.

Olga usually comforted Max, but she held her ground and stared at him, her expression frozen, her eyes bloodshot, her cheeks damp. William touched Max's arm. Their traumatised friend flinched the first time, but let him touch him when he tried again.

William led him back through to his own personal room. He sat him on his bed. If he'd had words for him, he would have offered them. Instead, he patted his shoulder and left.

While staring at the floor, her arms crossed over her chest, Olga waited for William to close Max's door before she said, "He probably needs the time on his own."

She needed the time on her own. And who could blame her? With Max's current state, she obviously didn't have as much of a burden to bear as him, but she had to hold the space for him to deal with his issues.

Crack! Whoosh! Dianna left the room into another one of the private pods.

A knock at the main door cut through the quiet. "Come in," William said.

William lost his breath when a hulking man filled their doorway. But the light caught Jan's grey hair. Father and son might have shared a similar silhouette, but Jan entered with humility and a smile. Maybe Aus would find his way to the same humble demeanour with time. The man cleared his throat, the force of his large diaphragm going off in the room like a firing cannon. "I've not had a proper chance to thank you all for bringing my little girl back to me."

"Not so little, Dad." Gracie stepped from behind him.

A glint in his eyes, crow's feet spread away from them with his smile. "You'll always be my baby."

Gracie tutted and dropped her attention to the floor.

"Anyway," Jan said, "thank you for bringing her back to me. And thank you for bringing back the solar panels. Our society can't operate without them. Oh, and don't mind Aus. He has a good heart. He cares a lot about this community, which can make him a bit …" Jan clicked his tongue and looked up at the ceiling as if seeking inspiration.

"Of a dick?" Olga said.

Jan smiled. "*Zealous* in his defence of the community. But he means no one any harm."

William raised his eyebrows at Tilly.

"You're welcome to stay here for as long as you like," Jan said. "I wanted to make sure you know that. Now, come on, love." He pulled on Gracie's arm. "Your friends look tired. Sleep well."

Crack! Jan hit the button beside the door. *Whoosh!* The door opened to let him out.

"You know," William said when the door closed, "Jan's right about all of us being tired. For now, Max needs time, and he needs our support. Artan?"

Matilda's brother had retreated into the shadows and sat on his bed. He looked William's way.

"Are you okay to run with Aus' crew for a while? At least if you're out with him, it'll keep him off my back."

"I'm the reason Edin fell." Artan stood up from his bed.

Matilda shook her head. "Hugh's the reason Edin fell, not you."

"However you look at it, I want to do my part to make sure Dout endures."

Hawk pressed his lips tight and glared at Artan like he wanted to murder him.

Matilda slipped her hand into William's. They slotted together like they were made to fit. She led him to another one of the private rooms and opened the door with a button press. *Whoosh!*

The small rooms had one double bed and a door on either side. Once the door had closed behind William, Matilda pressed a button to turn the locks on both doors red. She smiled as she stepped close to him. "If we're going to be here for a while, we might as well make good use of this chance to be alone."

For the first time since they'd been in Dout, William smiled. "Silver linings … And no one can come in?"

"No," Matilda said. "I checked with Gracie, and she said we can lock ourselves in here. Also"—she pointed at the door opposite the one they'd just walked through—"there's no one in that communal dorm."

"So we can sneak out of here whenever we want, and no one will notice."

Matilda smiled.

"You're right," William said, "we'll get out of here soon enough. Until then, we should probably make the most of this." He kissed Matilda, wrapped his arm around her lower back, and pulled her towards him.

CHAPTER 8

Max held her close and leaned into the warmth of their touching cheeks. They spun together, entwined, locked in a dance only they knew. They became one. He just needed physical contact. If only he'd worked that out sooner. For the first time since arriving in Dout, his mind stilled and his heart calmed.

Their steps mirrored one another's. Where he held her tight, she held him even tighter. She whispered in his ear.

"I'm sorry," Max said, "I didn't hear that."

She whispered again. Hoarse, as if she didn't have enough air in her lungs.

Max halted. He pulled back. "Oh, shit!"

The same rasping whisper. It came from deep within her. It slithered past her cracked lips. The downpour had turned her long and greasy hair lank. Strands of it stuck to her face, cutting black lines through her crimson glare. What teeth she had left were yellow pegs embedded in black gums. Her hoarse wheeze came not from her flapping mouth, but from the festering tear in her throat.

"No!" Max shoved her.

She turned and ran. She'd been fighting to get away the whole time. She tripped and landed on her knees.

Max chased after her, the ground slick.

The creature scrambled to her feet.

With one sweep, he cleaned her legs out, and she fell again. He kicked her in the face, tearing the gash in her throat wider. It left her staring at the sky, the back of her head resting between her shoulder blades. The chasm in her neck hissed. Her black tongue poked from her mouth like a reptile from a small dark crevice. She stared crimson fury at the heavens.

Max kicked her again. This time he brought his foot around from the side, connected with her ear with a *clop,* and tore her head clean from her shoulders.

The decapitated head bit at the air.

His face tacky with the diseased's bloody mucus, Max dragged some rainwater across his cheek and wiped it clean. He picked up the snapping head by her dank black hair and swung it like a slingshot before launching it away from him with a cry, "Yeargh!"

It struck another diseased just above its ear with a *tonk!*

Surrounded by the creatures. They were aimless in their wanderings. Some of them walked in circles as if they had one foot nailed to the ground.

"Yeargh!" Max charged at one, punched it, and knocked it on its back.

Like the woman he'd danced with, it snarled and hissed. It chewed the air, and its feet slipped in the mud with its desperate retreat.

Max climbed on top of it and punched it in the centre of its face. The thing's nose crunched beneath his attack. It twisted and writhed. It growled and gurned. It shook beneath him, snapping one way and then the other. He punched it again.

Weaponless, Max punched again and again. The creature's face distorted first, and then with each subsequent blow, he changed the shape of its skull. He gagged from its rotten stench, and his hand throbbed like he'd been punching rock.

Max's tears mixed with the rain. His throat burned with his torn cries. "You horrible fucks." He punched it again. "You think I fear you? Well, I don't. I won't let you beat me."

On his next blow, Max broke through the front of the creature's face. His fist sank into its nose with a squelch. He sat back and panted, his breaths ragged. These things wouldn't fucking scare him any longer. He wouldn't—

"Mum?" He threw himself off the creature and scrambled to his feet. He might have beaten the familiarity from its face, but she wore his mum's favourite dress. "I thought it was a man. Oh, Mum, I'm so sorry."

Max backed away, tripped over the body he'd rendered headless, and landed in a puddle of mud. "I'm so sorry."

The surrounding creatures watched him. His dad, his brothers, Cyrus, Hugh, Monica. All of them with their canted stances. They judged him. What the fuck had he just done?

The rain hit Max like falling gravel. He turned on the spot. Too dark to see farther than a few feet in each direction. "Where am I?" He threw his arms in the air. "Where am I?"

A light shone from a square hole in the ground. Max ran over to it on weary legs. A ladder embedded in the wall led down into a tunnel about thirty feet below. He sat at its edge, the mud soaking through his trousers. Hanging his legs down, he reached out with his right foot, feeling for a rung.

Once inside, Max reached up for the hatch and pulled it across. He turned the handle, locking it shut.

At the bottom of the ladder, the steel tunnel stretched out

ahead of him. He'd shut out the rain, but it still rang in his ears. "What was I playing at? How did I end up here?"

The end of the tunnel was in sight down the long and straight corridor. He quickened his pace. Whatever happened, he needed to get back into Dout unseen. Why had he gone outside on his own?

A diseased snapped at him in his mind. And then another one. They strobed through his thoughts, biting at him before vanishing back into the darkness.

"No." Max rapped his knuckles against his skull. "You won't win this. Whatever happens, you'll get out of my head."

His dad this time. Snarling and snapping. The face stayed longer than before. The bloody stare, usually hard to read, spoke of sadness and disappointment. What had become of his son?

A face appeared at the small square window in the door, and Max jumped back. His heart sank. "Oh, fuck!"

Whoosh! The door opened, and Gracie pointed at her temple. "What the fuck's wrong with you?"

"I … I … I was …"

"What can you possibly say that would justify what you've just done? *No one* goes outside on their own. Especially in your state."

The words forced Max back several steps. But what could he say? He'd lost his fucking mind. "I'm s—"

"Sorry?" Gracie laughed. "You're *fucking* sorry? Where will sorry get us when this place is overrun?"

"When?"

"If." Gracie shook her head and checked behind her. The lights in Dout were dulled. Most people would be in their rooms asleep. She reached out and pulled him through the door. "Come with me. We can't stay here. We need to get you cleaned up." After a moment, she added, "What did you expect to happen when you came back?"

"What do you mean?"

"How did you expect to get back in? A guard has to open the door for you. Did you think they wouldn't ask you questions?"

But he didn't remember going out. She didn't need to hear that. "I thought I might be able to blag my way back in."

Crack! Gracie slapped the button to open the door. She stepped aside to let him in. Her tone softened. "You need to get it together, Max. We all appreciate what you've done for us, and the toll it's taken on you, but when your actions are endangering an entire community …"

They were in Gracie's room. Half the size of Max's communal dorm, she had her own bed, desk, and shower in the corner.

Gracie sniffed in his direction. "You fucking stink." She pulled a curtain across her shower to give him privacy. "Clean yourself up. I'll get you some fresh clothes."

Max shivered as he undressed on the other side of the curtain. The door whooshed from where Gracie left. Maybe he should go now. Run and leave this community behind. He'd become a liability. He'd get everyone killed if he didn't get his shit together. The group would be better without him. He picked up his sodden trousers and tried to put them back on, but the damp fabric gripped his foot and wouldn't let go. He sat down on the cold steel floor and tried again. His legs and trousers were too wet. Steam filled the room from the hot shower. It took his diseased stink and forced it upon him. A stench that had been imprinted in his nostrils since they'd left Edin.

After wrestling his top off and dropping it onto the cold floor with a squelch, Max stepped into the hot shower. So hot it stung.

Whoosh! The door opened again.

"I've left your uniform just inside the curtain."

Enshrouded in steam, Max called back, "Thank you."

⁓

"So what were you playing at?" Gracie sat on her bed while Max dried his hair.

"I dunno." The start of tears itched his tired eyes. And then it came to him. Another flashback. This one useful. He'd snuck from his private room via the empty dorm on the other side. "I'm a liability to everyone. I wanted to fix that. I wanted to face the diseased. Desensitise myself so I can cope with going outside again. Everyone needs me to get better so we can move on."

Gracie shook her head and sighed. "But they're prepared to give you time."

"How did you know I'd gone out? Do the others know?"

Another shake of her head, Gracie said. "I was in the surveillance room. I saw you on the cameras."

"It's been recorded?"

"I deleted it."

Max pressed his hands together, palm to palm. "Thank you."

"Don't thank me yet. I'm not sure I made the correct decision, and I might still tell Dad. I think there was someone outside watching you. Someone from another community."

"You think?"

"It was dark out. I can't be sure."

"So what do we do?"

"*We* don't do anything. You go back to your room and get your head together. I don't know what I'm going to do yet. What I know is if Dad and Aus find out, you're dead."

"Will you at least give me a heads-up so I can get out of here?"

Tight-lipped, her brow locked in a scowl, Gracie shook

her head. "I don't know. I don't know what I'll do." She stood up. "Let's get you back to your room before anyone else notices you've gone walkabout."

The words delivered a gut punch. Gone walkabout like he was a senile old man they couldn't trust. Like an escapee from an asylum. A first-class liability. Maybe he should hand himself in. Let Aus do to him what he didn't have the balls to do to himself.

Whoosh! Gracie opened the door and stepped out into the hallway.

Max followed.

∾

THE DORM on the other side of their private rooms lay empty. They had just over two hundred and fifty people in this community, but they could accommodate many more.

Gracie led him into the room and stood aside. "Which pod is yours?"

Max pointed at the door leading to his private room. He led Gracie over to it. She laid a hand on his shoulder and forced eye contact. "Look, I can see what you're going through. I can only guess at how hard it is to live with. Let's hope there's no comeback from what happened tonight. Let's hope we got away with it, yeah? And let's not talk about it. If I cover this up and Aus and Dad find out, they'll be as pissed with me as they will be with you." For the first time that night, she smiled.

He smiled back. "I'm sorry." Max pressed the button to open his door. His smile fell instantly. "Olga?"

She stood in his room, her hands on her hips. Her eyes ran from Max to Gracie and back again. "W-what …? What's happening? What's going on?" She grew quieter. "What have you two been up to?"

CHAPTER 9

Artan ducked when a fish twice his size swam past. His mouth hung open, and despite being in the pleasure dome for the past hour, he remained in awe of the immersive experience. He could have spent an entire day in there and he would have found new things to look at. The colours of the fish and plant life were unlike any he'd ever seen. They'd been told the footage they used in the pleasure dome came from actual places. That it had all been recorded with no added effects.

Matilda stood to Artan's left, Max to his right. Despite his resentment towards Artan, Hawk had come along with them, as had William and Olga. He'd spent the entire time staring at him from beneath his thick brow.

"I don't know where this place is," Artan said, "but I want to go."

When no one replied, Artan said, "Anyone?"

Soothing music played through the large domed room. They shared the space with several other small groups. Each of them stood huddled together and threw the occasional glance at Artan and his friends.

Artan shook his head and threw his arms up in a shrug. "Good chat!"

Hawk's fury made sense, but something had gone on with Olga and Max. She stood as far away from him as she could while remaining a part of their group.

They'd spent most of the day in their room, dozing and catching up on rest. Artan, Hawk, and Olga had remained in the communal space, where one awkward silence morphed into the next. It had been broken occasionally by Matilda and William's giggles from their pod. At least some of them were having fun. Max had also locked himself away, and who knew where Dianna had gone.

"So," Artan tried again, a shoal of orange fish with white stripes passing him on his right. His fingers twitched with a desire to reach out and touch them. "How's everyone's day been?"

William giggled. Both Hawk and Olga shot him glares.

"Max?"

Bags like fat slugs hung beneath Max's eyes. Thick white bands ran beneath his irises as if the lower half of his face weighed more than his muscles could support. He watched the room through a glazed stare.

"Ol—"

She raised an eyebrow at him. Address her directly and she'd take his fucking head off. He pulled a tight-lipped smile at Hawk, who raised his top lip in a snarl.

Whoosh! The door to the pleasure dome opened, and Gracie entered. She waved and grinned. Were Olga wound any tighter by the time she reached them, she would have shattered. "Hi, guys!"

"I'm not a guy," Olga said.

"I'm sorry, you're right."

Olga sneered.

Another wide smile, Gracie said, "How are you all?"

Max lowered his head. Hawk remained fixed on Artan. William and Matilda smiled. Olga said, "Fuck off, Gracie."

"Hey!" Matilda said. "There's no need for that."

"There's every fucking need," Olga said.

Gracie batted the comment away. "It's fine. Honestly. I want to take you outside tonight. I have a few jobs I need to do, and figure you could get another look at the wall."

"I'm not going anywhere with you," Olga said.

"We will." William held hands with Matilda.

Gracie paused for a few seconds. When Hawk refused even eye contact, her smile faltered. "Right," she said, "I'll come to your room and get you."

"They're in a private room," Olga said. "You know all about sneaking into them, eh?"

Max's already stooped head lowered further.

Artan raised an eyebrow. Did Olga want to explain? Her tight eyes suggested she didn't. In fact, push her and she'd take his fucking head off.

As Gracie departed, Hawk muttered to himself, "I'm not going out on one of those shitty missions. Fuck this place. They can do their own dirty work. Fuck them." His dark eyes narrowed, and he pointed at Artan. "You should have let me fight my own battle when we went out there."

"Shut the fuck up, Hawk." Olga rolled her eyes and shook her head. "Even if your ego didn't want to be saved, he had a responsibility to Dianna. You put her in danger, and from where I was standing, you had no fucking idea her life was under threat."

"I—"

Aus entered the pleasure dome and marched towards them, his wide shoulders hunched, his jaw jutting from his large face. A shark swam alongside him. He pointed his thick index finger at Artan. "I want to see you in the surveillance room in fifteen minutes. We're going out tonight."

"Take me with you," Hawk said. The rage had gone. The scowl had lifted. "Give me a chance to show you what I can do. I'm a hunter. I've been hunting much longer than Artan. You could do with me on your team. You won't regret it."

"Even if you'd been perfect." Aus leaned forward and lowered his voice as if sharing a secret with him. "And trust me, you were nowhere near perfect, then I still wouldn't have chosen you to run with my team."

The strain of Hawk's whine turned his voice high-pitched. "Why?"

"Those scars around your neck."

Hawk's face fell as slack as Max's. He touched his neck as if feeling the scars for the first time. "This was done to me when I was a child."

"Not *those* scars. The rope burns."

Artan gasped.

Hawk opened his mouth, but Aus cut him off. "You know what those scars tell me? They tell me you're not fit to run with us. When you're deep in enemy territory, you need to keep your head. You need to be able to fight. Those scars show me what you do when the chips are down. We need soldiers, not quitters."

Tears filled Hawk's eyes, and he clenched his quivering jaw. "You have no idea—"

"Maybe I don't, but I need to pick someone I can rely on."

"You want someone with fight?" A single tear ran down Hawk's left cheek. His voice broke, and he jabbed a thumb at his own chest. "I fought every single day. I fought the voices and the torment. I fought the memories. I wouldn't mind betting that by the time I was eight, I'd been through more than you've experienced in your entire life. What I had to deal with is harder than fighting diseased or running through hostile communities. You know what"—more tears flowed—"you're lucky you can't understand what I've been through. Your lack of empathy speaks of your privilege, not of my will."

"Maybe." Aus shrugged. "But am I prepared to take the risk?" He shook his head, and his features darkened. His deep voice boomed through the pleasure dome. "No." And then to Artan, he said, "See you in the surveillance room in fifteen."

As Aus walked off, Hawk rubbed his tears away with the back of his right hand, dragging his face with the hard pull.

"What he just said then was out of order." Artan shook his head. "I want no part in that."

The same rage he'd levelled on Artan all day returned to Hawk's features.

"I'm going to tell Aus I don't want to run with him."

"Fuck off, Artan."

"What?"

"Don't be so fucking condescending."

Some people from the other groups looked over at Hawk's raised voice. "You've already taken this away from me. Don't take away my agency over fighting my own battles. You're not here to save me, so just leave me the fuck alone, okay?"

Matilda reached over and squeezed the back of Artan's hand while Hawk left the pleasure dome.

A few seconds after he'd gone, Olga did the same, Max following when she'd vanished from sight.

Matilda said, "You coming back to the room?"

Artan shook his head. "I'd rather not. I need to get my thoughts straight before I go out with Aus and his crew. I think Hawk needs some time away from me, too. You be careful when you go out with Gracie, yeah?"

William patted Artan's shoulder. "You too, man. See you in the morning."

After Matilda and William left, Artan turned slow circles

to take in the fish. The ceiling shone brightest from where the sun's light hit the water's surface far above them. A fish, black but with a silvery shine, and about three feet long, zipped through the slower movers. The silhouette of a hammerhead shark passed overhead. It looked like an alien spacecraft and threw a temporary shadow over the room.

Artan jumped at the hand on his shoulder.

Nick had a brilliant white smile. His deep brown eyes were as dark as his skin.

"Where did you come from?"

He pointed to another group of people on the other side of the room. "I was chilling out over there. It's a good place to come when you want to wind down." The shimmering light from the surrounding water reflected off the side of his bald head. "Although, you lot didn't look very chilled."

"You saw all of that?"

"Yeah. What's going on?"

Artan laughed. "I don't know. Something's happened between Olga, Max, and Gracie. Hawk's blaming me for saving his life. And William and Matilda—" he shook his head as if he could banish the thought "—well, they're about the only ones having a good time."

Nick raised his eyebrows. "At least someone's getting it."

Artan laughed.

Flicking his head in the direction of the pleasure dome's exit, Nick said, "How about we go to the surveillance room early?"

Artan smiled and lowered his voice. "I'd like that. It kinda feels like I'm centre stage in here."

"You get used to it," Nick said. "It's a good community, but privacy is hard to come by. Especially when you're having such public arguments, and when you're as new as you lot."

Artan laughed. "We didn't help ourselves, eh?"

Nick patted him on the back and walked towards the exit. "Come on, let's go."

CHAPTER 10

William walked on the spot, his feet squelching in the muddy ground. A light shone from the open hatch behind them. Another exit from Gracie's community. She closed it, and it vanished into the landscape, the top covered in small mossy rocks like those around it. Dout had gone to a lot of effort to remain hidden. No wonder they were so zealous in their protection of it.

Gracie scanned their surroundings and rolled her shoulders. She leaned forward ever so slightly. The straps of her backpack were taut from the load. A spear in her hand and a sword in a hilt at her side. William and Matilda both carried swords.

"It's good to be outside," William said. Matilda frowned at him. He acknowledged her glare with a nod and lowered his voice before saying to Gracie, "It's tense back in our room. Hawk's pissed with Artan. Max is a loose cannon. Olga's—"

"Olga," Gracie said.

A slight smile, William said, "Right."

"Did Aus really need to say that to Hawk?" Matilda said.

"Aus is a dick. He's my brother, and I should love him, but I don't. Were it not for Dad, I'd have nothing to do with him."

"Should I pass that warning on to Artan?" Matilda said.

"The thing with Aus," Gracie said, "is he doesn't do subtle. So if he's gunning for you, you know."

William snorted. "Tell me about it."

"Also," Gracie said, "of all of us, I think Artan's in the best position to be on his good side. That brotherhood of his. His *soldiers*"—she rolled her eyes—"mean more to him than anything. Sure, he'll put him through his paces, but as long as he passes the tests, he'll be tighter than family. He'll also ease up on everyone else. He's always the hardest on new people."

"I'm not sure we'll ever get to see another side of him," William said.

"You still planning on leaving soon?"

When Matilda didn't intervene, William nodded. "As soon as we can. We just need Max to get his shit together."

Gracie's cheeks reddened at the mention of Max. "I used to take it personally, you know."

"What?" Matilda said.

"Aus. How he is. His constant attacks and nastiness." She winced; her voice tightened. "Living with him day in and day out. It kind of … gets to you after a while."

"I can imagine." Matilda rubbed the top of Gracie's arm, and although the girl tensed, she didn't move away. "Did your dad not get involved?"

Gracie cleared her throat. "I think he finds it hard. It took me a while to make sense of it because I was so preoccupied with the injustice of it all, but I can see now that he genuinely loves us both the same. And because of that, how can he pick a side?"

"Surely that's easier when one of you is clearly in the right?" William said.

Gracie shrugged. "He doesn't have that objectivity, so he

stays out of it. Also, it helps to see how Aus is with other people. He's not just an arsehole to me. It's his problem, not mine."

A silence that needed filling, William said, "So what's going on with you, Max, and Olga?"

Something snarled on their right. A low rumble. Creatures in the shadows. Gracie spun towards the sound, her spear raised.

Several diseased descended on them, their clumsy steps hammering an irregular beat.

One of them, the front runner, broke from the pitch black as a dark silhouette. Three more behind it. Two more after that. Six of them in total. They could deal with six.

Thwip! Gracie launched her spear. It hit the first diseased in the face with a *schlock!* The force of her attack drove the creature back, knocking it into the three behind. All four went down like she'd struck the kingpin.

William and Matilda followed Gracie towards the beasts. She drove her sword through the face of the creature she'd speared. She ripped it out with a squelch and threw a hacking slash at the neck of the next diseased.

Matilda overtook William, stuck the tip of her sword into one of the three fallen, and continued without breaking stride into the other two. Two sharp stabbing lunges, one to the face of each, they both crumpled like they'd been turned off.

Only one left. The moonlight revealed the fresh glistening wound on the side of its face. Yet to be withered by the disease, it lay pinned beneath one of its dead crew. It snarled, twisted, and turned. An involuntary sneer lifted the right side of William's face. One mistake and he'd be one of them, or even worse, he'd lose Matilda to the vile disease.

Squelch! Gracie drove the end of her sword into the creature's right eye. She pulled it out again, drawing a line of blood between the beast and the sword's tip. She cupped her ear. "Hear that?"

It took a few seconds. Distant snarls rode the wind. The swishing of long grass.

"Come on," Gracie said. "Let's get out of here."

∽

THEY ARRIVED at a cluster of ruined houses via an old road. Grass grew through the cracks in the asphalt. The house closest to them had been the most devastated. What remained of its walls stood about a foot tall. A guide for what had once been there.

The houses farther back grew progressively taller, leading all the way to some that still had their roofs. The low broken wall in front of them provided the perfect stepping stone. Gracie led the climb.

The wall a foot wide, she walked up the steep incline with the grace of a squirrel along a tree branch. Of course, Matilda followed her, her pace no different to when she'd been on the ground. She glanced back at William, but when he scowled at her, she minded her own business. He'd get there eventually.

Tired from the run, adrenaline flooding his system, William climbed only four feet from the ground before he lost his balance and fell, boosting away from the wall to avoid the fallen rubble gathered around its base. Land on that and he'd break an ankle.

"Are you—"

William glared at Matilda again. He didn't need her help.

Past the point where he fell, William remained upright. He could have crawled, but the girls hadn't. Although, would he be more of an embarrassment if they needed to carry him and his shattered ankles back to Dout?

Ten feet from the ground, William pushed on. His pulse spiked when he stepped on a wobbly brick. He fell forward onto the wall, the rough brickwork grazing his palms. Matilda's attention burned into the top of his head, but he refused to look up.

Gracie had already gotten to work by the time William reached the pitched roof at the top. They were now twenty feet up. The solar panels had been impossible to see from the ground. Six in total, each one clipped to the next. They were about half the size of the ones they'd stolen the previous evening.

Slipping her bag from her shoulders, Gracie rested it on the roof, undid the zip, and pulled out another tile. She clipped it to the end of those already there. From her bag, she also pulled two small metal bricks.

William took them for her. They were cold to touch. "What are these?"

"Batteries." Gracie reached under the roof and pulled a similar metal block out and handed it to Matilda. "Back in the day, we used to have massive batteries. What we're doing now would have been a four- or five-man job. We couldn't put them in a bag or in our pockets." She sighed and shook her head before reaching under the roof again. "We lost many people because of the burden of those things."

After handing Matilda the second battery from beneath the roof, she pulled a pair of binoculars from her bag and gave them to William. She took the batteries from him and pointed into the darkness.

The silhouette of the wall stretched across the landscape. Too dark to get the finer details, but the binoculars still brought the image closer. The moon ran a silver highlight along its brushed steel surface. How the hell were they supposed to get over that?

"That's us done," Gracie said. She slipped from the wall

and hung down before dropping to what remained of this house's first floor.

Matilda followed, landing like a cat.

Flat-footed, William landed next to them. *Thud.* "Why don't you put a ladder he—"

"Shh!" Gracie pressed a finger to her lips.

Several seconds later, the phlegmy, choking rattle reached William. He copied the other two by stepping back into the shadows.

A diseased ran across the back of the ruins. A lone creature, it moved on the edge of its balance. Its right arm hung loose and swung with its momentum. The darkness soon swallowed its awkward silhouette.

"If we put a ladder here," Gracie said, "someone will climb it and find our solar panels. We survive because of hidden spots like this. We also have small gardens dotted all over the place. It's a lot of work, but it makes us less vulnerable if they're found, and it also makes us seem like a much smaller community than we are." She pointed down. "It's rocky on the ground, so be careful." She lowered herself from the first floor and dropped.

Once again, Matilda hit the ground with a ten-point-zero landing. William didn't break his ankles. That's the best he could hope for.

∾

The wall loomed large on their left. Diseased screams called through the night. None were close enough to be a threat.

Gracie dropped into a hunch and opened her bag.

"Why are we stopping here?" William said.

She handed both him and Matilda binoculars before she moved a bush aside and pulled a carrot from the ground.

"Like I said, we have to farm and collect power subtly. Take this moment to look at the wall."

"It looks so different at night," Matilda said.

"Although," William snorted, "I'm not sure seeing the thing in all its glory during the day has filled me with hope for how we're going to get past it."

A sheer face of brushed steel. About two hundred feet tall. The guns sat as uniform lumps along the top. The moon shone on several guards. They either stood at ease or paced up and down the small space above the gates. The only part of the wall to have a patrol.

"Right," Gracie said, "let's move on." Her bag as full now as it had been when they'd left Dout.

"That was quick," Matilda said.

"You learn to be when you've done it enough times."

"You know," William said, "you've still not told us what's going on with you, Olga, and—"

The caterwauling siren rang out. The top of the wall glowed red with the spinning lights. *Clunk!* The gates opened. "We can't stay here," Gracie said. "Especially not in the dark."

"How the hell are we going to get over the wall?" William said.

Gracie shrugged. "If I knew, I'd tell you." She bounced on her toes. "But we can't stay here. We need to go via the river on the way home to get water. At least we know where all the diseased and the people from the other communities will be heading."

"Why do the other communities come here?"

"Because they know the people being evicted."

"Do they ever evict people like us?"

"'That sound like us?" Gracie said.

"Yeah."

"I can't tell you for sure, but in all my time here, I've never seen it."

"I'm guessing they're evicting their enemies from the gates. And, if they don't sound like us, does that mean we're not their enemies?"

"Who knows?" Gracie said. "Although, the other communities hate us with all their being, so it would certainly make sense." She paused. Dogs barked in the distance. "But we still have to get moving. Come on."

˜

The cold water stung William's hands, and they tingled on their way to turning numb, hindering his attempts to screw the lid back on. Matilda and Gracie had already filled their water bladders and wore them on their backs.

"Max is your best bet for getting past the wall," Gracie said. "We all know what he can do—"

"You won't tell the others in your community?" Matilda said.

"No." Gracie shook her head. "But, as for getting you past that wall, he's nowhere near ready to do what you need of him. And he might never be. I found him in a state last night. I helped him. That's why Olga's pissed with me. She got the wrong impression and got jealous."

"So how long do you reckon we'll have to wait for Max to get himself together?" William said. "I told him to take his time, but there has to be a limit."

Gracie's lips tightened. "I'm not sure. He's seen a lot of shit. Who knows? What if he never comes back from this?"

William exhaled, his cheeks puffing out. "I've been trying to avoid asking that question."

CHAPTER 11

They called him Mad Max. The crazy one. The wild one. The one who moved through life without thought like a whirlwind, leaving only destruction in his wake. Whatever that meant. But he had a side they didn't see. He could be quiet. He could hide. He could hide better than any of them. He'd show them. He climbed the tree while Greg counted.

"Ninety-eight. Ninety-nine. One hundred." Greg uncovered his eyes. "Coming, ready or not."

There were other kids in the park, and several of them had seen where Max went. They'd best keep their mouths shut.

Greg walked beneath the tree, but Max had climbed higher than ever before. He clung to the branch and held his breath. If his mum saw him now, she'd have a fit.

"Gotcha!" Greg shouted.

"Argh!" Sam crawled from beneath a bush and walked back to the swings, passing beneath Max. He didn't see him either. They had no chance of finding him. They'd have to admit defeat eventually.

Greg, the oldest boy in the family, didn't play with them often. And when he did, he always won. But not today. Max clamped his hand across his mouth to contain his laughter.

"Gotcha!" Greg found Matthew.

"That's not fair!" Matthew said. "You peeked when you were counting."

Greg laughed. "Like I needed to cheat to find your shit hiding place."

"You cheated."

"You're out, Matthew. Stop moaning."

Just Drake left to find now. Even if Greg found Max, if he found him last, that would be the best. Being the youngest, he never won at anything.

From his spot near the top of the tree, Max had seen where everyone went. His small heart hammered when Greg got close to Drake's hiding place. He'd jumped over a hedge and hid on the other side. But, being winter, there were no leaves on the bush. Even Max had a line of sight on him.

"Gotcha!" Greg laughed as the red-faced Drake stood up. "You lot make it too easy."

"Not me." Max giggled. "You'll never find me."

"Come on." Greg threw an arm around Drake. "Let's go home."

Max giggled again and spoke beneath his breath. "Nice try, Greg. I know what you're doing, but it won't work. You can pretend to leave me as much as you want. I won't show you where I'm hiding."

Hard to contain his laughter, Max kept his hand across his mouth as both Greg and Drake passed beneath the tree. Greg still had his arm around his little brother. They joined up with Matthew and Sam at the swings.

All of them pretended to be in on the trick. All of them walked away together, back toward their house. But they wouldn't fool Max. They'd have to admit he'd won before he came down.

∽

MAX SHIVERED, the winter wind cutting through him. At least two hours had passed since Greg and the others left the park. Day had turned to night. The park had fallen quiet. Why hadn't they come back for him? Were they that reluctant to admit he'd won?

"Greg?" Max said. His voice echoed through the empty park. He tried a little louder. "Greg?" They had to be hiding somewhere, waiting for him to come down. They wouldn't leave him here on his own. Would they? What would their mum say? At five, she always said Max shouldn't be going anywhere alone.

Max's knees hurt from where he'd crouched in the tree. They bore the frigid blast of the wind. He hung one leg down and swung it to ease some of his aches. He hung the next leg down to do the same. He'd have to go home soon. His mum and dad would be worried. But, if they were worried, why hadn't they come looking for him?

Max clung onto a branch across from him and swung down. He trembled, his thin trousers and top useless against the cold. His bottom lip buckled. They might have thought they were being funny, but they weren't.

The lowest branch about six feet from the ground, Max hung from it, his belly exposed from where his top rode up. Drake's old top and Sam's before him. He let go, landed, and fell to his knees in the mud.

The fabric on the front of his trousers now sodden. What would his mum say when he got home? They were clean on that morning. He'd never been out this late on his own before. He'd never seen the park empty. One last try, Max shouted, "Greg?"

His echo ran away from him.

He sprinted home.

∽

Gasping by the time he reached his door, Max snapped the handle down and fell into his front room. His family sat around the table, eating their dinner. He sweated, his nose and ears stinging from the cold. He panted and pointed a finger at Greg. "You left me."

Red-faced with laughter, Greg remained locked in a conversation with their dad. "And, of course, Matthew said I'd cheated."

Their dad winked at Matthew. "Always dignified in defeat, eh, son?"

Matthew sat back in his chair and folded his arms.

Max stepped forward and threw his skinny arms wide. "But *I* won! He couldn't find me. He had to go home."

"So who was the last one out?" Max's mum said. None of them had looked at Max.

"Me!" Max stamped his foot. "I was the last one out. I was still in the game, and you all went home. You all left me."

If they heard him, they hid it well.

Max stamped his foot again. "Hey! I'm here. I said I won! I was the last one out! I was—"

Darkness smothered Max. A sheet over his head. He twisted and turned. He kicked it away, but it clung to his damp skin, wrapping him tighter until he finally wrestled it free. He shouted, "I was the last one out. I'm here!"

Olga stood in the doorway of his room, her jaw hanging loose.

"I'm—" The words left him. The last one out. The last man standing. The only one still alive. His throat burned. His eyes itched. Using his sheet to wipe away his sweat, he swallowed a dry gulp. He bit his bottom lip and shook his head. "Oh, Olga."

Olga sat down on the bed next to Max and put an arm around him. "It's okay, honey. You're okay. Everything's going to be fine."

"I'm not sure it is." Max shook his head. "It doesn't feel like it'll be fine." Had he killed the children in the dining hall? Had he compromised Dout by going outside? Unable to tell the difference between reality and his imagination, everything felt very fucking far from okay.

"And not only might I never be okay again, but everyone's waiting for me to get better. William, Matilda, and Hawk all want to leave already." He shook his head. Tears stung his eyes. "I'm not ready to leave. Nowhere near it."

"They're adults," Olga said. "They need to make their own choices, just like you need to make yours. Just like I need to make mine. I'm here for you. And I'm sorry about how I reacted with Gracie. It's just … you know … it didn't look very good. You two together in the room; you having freshly showered."

"I told you what happened. She found me walking around the place. I didn't know where I was. The shower helped ground me. It brought me back."

"I know." Olga nodded. She looked away and stared into the middle distance. "I know."

"I feel so alone. I don't know what to do."

"I wish I could tell you." Olga kissed the top of his head. "I can't pretend to know how you're feeling, but I can promise you I'll be here for you. Whatever else happens, I'm by your side for as long as you need me, okay?"

A wave of tears surged through Max. "You're sure? I don't want to drag you down."

They lay back on the bed together and held one another. Olga kissed the top of Max's head again and said, "Life without you would drag me down. Whatever it takes, we'll get through this. You're tired. You need to rest."

CHAPTER 12

Artan and Nick ran side by side in the dark. They fell into step, finding their rhythm at the back of the pack. Aus led them with Freddie next to him. The rest of the crew ran in pairs between them. "This is going to take some getting used to," Artan said.

"What?" Nick said.

"This military life. Also, I've not had much rest over the past few months."

"You get time off during the day. My advice—" Nick drew a deep breath, the first sign the run was affecting him "— make the most of your downtime."

They ran through long grass. The damp blades soaked Artan's trousers. His feet sank with every step on the boggy ground.

A swish to his right, Artan halted and locked onto it. He launched his spear and hit the first diseased of the pack. The rest of the team attacked.

Nick threw his spear and smiled. "You're a fast learner."

Artan shrugged. "I get the feeling that if I don't learn fast, I'll die."

The diseased down, Artan joined the others in retrieving his spear.

Where most leaders would have praised him, Aus locked on Artan. The man stood taller and wider than him. In that moment he grew an extra few inches. Pointing a thick sausage finger, he said, "Don't get cocky because you had a lucky break. To prove you have what it takes to run with my crew, you have to do a hell of a lot more than see a diseased in the dark."

They set off again, Artan and Nick waiting for the other four pairs to lead the way.

"Is he always like that?" Artan said.

"Yeah. Especially with rookies. It might seem harsh, but he will ease up. And the rest of us are grateful to have you. We're responsible for each other's lives out here. There's no room for fuck-ups."

"So I get your approval, then?"

"Of course. How are you finding Dout so far?"

Artan snorted. "It's a barrel of laughs. Max is losing his mind. Olga and Gracie want to murder one another. William and Matilda want to leave, and while they think they're putting no pressure on me—"

"They're putting pressure on you."

"Yep. And Tilly's my sister, so of course I'll go when she thinks the time's right."

"Do you think that'll be soon?"

"Depends on Max. At the moment, he seems like he needs a lot more time. And then there's Hawk. He used to be part of a hunting team." Artan waved a hand over their surroundings as if showing it to Nick. "This is what he does."

"But Aus selected you."

"And Hawk is livid. So, in answer to your question, things in Dout are pretty damn stressful. Coming out here and being attacked by diseased feels like a break from it all."

The others had reached the brow of a hill and stopped. Artan and Nick joined them. They overlooked another community. Unlike the one they'd already visited, this one had a steel wall surrounding it. The barrier stood as a miniature version of the one they were yet to cross. "Do you think we'll find a way over the main wall?"

Nick shook his head. Paused. And then said, "Maybe."

As if on cue, the siren wailed in the distance over to their right. The flashing lights threw splashes of crimson across the top of the imposing barrier. "Should we worry about that?"

Another shake of his head, Nick said, "It should benefit us. It will make some of this community head over there to see if they can rescue any of their own. We can slip in while they're distracted."

"Why doesn't Dout try to rescue the people who come through that wall?"

"Because all the people who come through don't speak the same language as us. However you feel about foreigners, they all hate us. Any attempt to help them will endanger our lives."

His middle and index finger on his right hand pressed together like rabbit ears, Aus flicked them toward the steel-walled community and led them on.

Artan and Nick reached the community last. Nothing compared to the wall they intended to climb, but still too sheer to scale.

"There are three rules you need to follow," Aus said.

How many times did he need to tell him this?

"One," Aus said. "Don't get caught or seen. Two, if you get caught or seen, don't run back to Dout. Three, if you are near Dout when you realise you're being followed, make sure you don't give the place away. Don't let our community fail because you fucked up. So far you've kept up, and you've shown you can spot a diseased in the darkness, but to run with my crew, you need to get over this challenge." Aus pulled back a bush at the base of the wall. A small tunnel had been dug beneath the steel. "You lead the way."

Artan slipped off his spear sheath and leaned it against the wall. He kept his empty bag on his back and checked the knife at his hip. The only defence he'd have against trouble. He lay on his front in the slimy mud and slithered into the small tunnel.

The echo of his own breaths mocked him in the tight space. He grunted and snorted, using his elbows to drag him towards the faint light. The tunnel had a gradual decline, levelled out, and then rose again. Only a short distance, but the tight press, and the fact that tonnes of steel could come crashing down on him, made it ten times the length.

The tunnel's exit faced another steel wall, giving Artan a gap about a foot wide. He slithered from the hole, clambered up onto his knees, and stood in the tight space. He moved aside for Aus to come through next. The man was twice his size, but he managed it in a fraction of the time and with infinitely more grace.

As the others came through, Artan moved sideways to accommodate Aus, who accommodated them. The smaller wall in front of them, only about three or four feet taller than Artan, was the back of a building. He shuffled along until he reached the spot where the large steel hut ended. He overlooked a pit, the ground about ten feet below. The gap they'd shuffled along between the wall and the hut continued as a one-foot-wide ledge along the back of the pit. Wide enough to walk along. Narrow enough to fall from.

Artan led them again. The second he stepped from the cover of the building, a wave of snarling and barking fury rushed at him. Dogs. At least fifty of them. They gathered below. Bared teeth. Saliva dripping from their jaws. They dared him to fall.

Artan pulled back behind the hut. "What the hell?"

Aus shoved him. "You need to move. Now. Dogs bark. That's not so much of an issue, but if you stay here too long, someone will come to check out what the fuss is about." He shoved Artan again, harder this time. "Go. Now."

His first few steps on adrenaline-shaking legs, Artan stumbled onto the ledge. The wall on one side, a fall into a pit filled with dogs on the other. He could do this. His attention on the path six feet ahead, he sped up, reached the other end of the ledge, and ran from the dog pit.

The closest building about fifty feet away, cuboid and with a pitched roof. Artan reached it and pressed his back to the wall. A small window beside him, the place lit by a single bulb. It contained supplies for the dog pit. Straw. Food. A broom. The outline of a door in one wall, but it had no handle. How did people get out of there if the door closed on them? The light glistened on a greasy patch on the left side of the door at waist height. While the others caught up, he took in the rest of the community. They'd built everything from steel. The houses, the wall, the larger buildings. Even the dog pit had steel walls and floor. The building they'd emerged behind, a steel kennel.

When the others caught up, Aus leaned close to Artan. "Slow down like that again, and I'll cut your throat."

Artan pressed his lips tight and, when Aus looked away, raised his eyebrows at Nick.

It made sense for them to enter the community from this side. There weren't many residential buildings close by. And understandably so. The place stank of dog shit, and the barking would drive anyone nuts.

At the edge of the building, Artan said, "How do they get into these huts? They don't have any door handles."

"We don't know," Aus said, "so don't get yourself trapped inside."

"That's happened?"

"No. And don't let it."

"But there must be a way out. Surely they don't hold their citizens hostage in their own homes?"

"I wouldn't put anything past these fucks. Not after what they did to Shah."

"Shah?"

"He was someone from my crew. They got a hold of him and … well, let's just say it would have been kinder for us to throw a spear through him as they dragged him off. Now come on, let's go."

Aus took the lead. Like in the previous community, he had the route mapped in his mind.

They passed the backs of the small cuboid buildings, stooping to avoid the windows, the lights on inside. The damp weather had turned the ground muddy, but, like with the previous community, they mostly stuck to the paths laid through the place.

Aus held his arm out to halt Artan, who'd run behind him the entire way. "That's their armoury," he said, pointing at a building ahead. Similar in size and shape to the barns they had back in Edin. It had a pitched roof and a grid of windows running up the side of one of its steel walls. "You need to find a way to get the ammo out of there."

"What?"

Nick leaned close to Artan. "Get onto the roof and use the chimney."

Aus shoved Nick back before he could tell Artan any more. He pointed at him and Jason, a skinny man in his early twenties. "You two stay on the ground and catch the ammo as we drop it." He slapped Artan on the back. "We don't have time to fuck about."

A quick check both ways, Artan led the rest of Aus' crew to the armoury. The windows were the obvious route. They were covered in steel bars and ran from the ground to the roof. He climbed, and Aus followed. The rest lined up and waited.

About fifteen feet from the ground, and at the highest window, Artan peered through the space over the top of the wall and beneath the roof. An obvious way in. But Nick had told him to use the chimney. And Aus had told him not to get caught inside. Not unless he wanted to end up like Shah.

The roof had a lip running along its edge. That had to be the way up. Artan grabbed it with his right hand and leaned away from the wall. He tugged on the lip, his stomach lurching. If he fell ... Hopefully someone would put him out of his misery if he broke his back.

Reaching up with his left hand, Artan squeezed, testing the lip. He kicked away from the wall, swung out, and dragged himself onto the roof with a pull-up.

Solar panels lined the roof. The lip must have been to stop them sliding off. Artan crawled across them to the chimney. Aus on his heels, Freddie behind him.

"What was Nick talking about?" Artan said.

Aus remained tight-lipped. He had to work it out himself.

Artan tapped the chimney on each of its four sides. The steel panels were welded together. The opening in the top too narrow to be useful. "What did he mean?"

Aus spoke in a growl. "You'd best work it out fast, rookie."

"Aus!" A man at the back of the line waved in their direction and pointed away from the barn. "People!"

Artan copied the others in dropping to his front. The solar panels were cold against his chest. The others lay still, but he shuffled up the roof and peered over. Aus would be pissed with him, so he didn't look back.

A crew of seven, a mix of men and women. They led a

pack of dogs and carried electric torches. They ran past the armoury. They must have been on their way to the wall's opening gates.

The building opposite them must have been a communal space. A hall with large windows. The shine from the guards' torches showed Artan a reflection of the armoury beneath him.

When they ran from view, Artan slid back down the solar panels, away from the chimney.

"What are you doing?" Aus said.

"Getting the ammo out of this place."

"Didn't you hear what Nick said?"

"I know he tried to help me." Artan reached the edge of the roof and gripped the steel lip. "But I don't know what he was talking about." He slipped backwards from the roof.

Hanging, Artan swung his legs under and caught the top of the steel wall with his ankles. He pulled himself in until he hooked over, the backs of his knees resting on the top of the wall. Letting go with his left hand, he grabbed next to his left leg. He pulled the rest of his body under so he sat, hunched in the tight space beneath the roof, a gargoyle overlooking a dark warehouse.

Artan's stomach turned backflips with every movement. The wall narrow, he turned around and hung down, catching the first window ledge with his right foot. He followed the path he'd taken to the roof back down to the ground. This time, inside the armoury. The place still. It reeked of metal. The taste of it lay along the back of his tongue like a nosebleed. "I hope this works." His voice echoed in the building, his steps snapping through the place when he went to the door he'd seen in the window's reflection. Handleless, like the others in the community.

While biting down on his bottom lip, Artan shoulder barged it. *Click!* It opened and swung wide.

The light from outside spilled into the place, illuminating the ammo supplies. Boxes and boxes of bullets. Guns like the ones Artan had seen in Dout's armoury. He didn't have the first clue on which ones he should take, but—

"Oh my!" Aus lay on the roof directly above Artan. He grinned for the first time since Artan had met him.

Nick and Jason, who'd waited on the ground, were the first to the door. "Well done," Nick said and ran into the building. He headed straight for the boxes of bullets and opened his bag beside them.

One after the other, Aus' crew ran into the armoury and either smiled at Artan or patted his back. Even Aus, as the last one in, dipped him a nod and said, "Well done, new kid. Well done."

CHAPTER 13

"You know what?" William leaned close to Matilda, the flimsy plastic chair squeaking beneath him. "At least it's been quiet these past few days. I didn't realise how much I've needed this rest."

Matilda smiled. "I'm sure it won't be long before Gracie takes us out on another night-time supply run."

"Enjoy the time off while we can get it, eh?"

Matilda shrugged.

They sat shoulder to shoulder with the other spectators in the sports hall. Seats surrounded the rectangular court. It had a polished wooden floor, an outline around the edge in white tape, and a centre line of the same colour bisecting the pitch. There were many gaps in the seating area. Even if everyone in Dout showed up for the game, there would still be as many spaces as there were people.

Artan entered the room with Nick. Both of them smiled and waved. The crowd applauded.

"Artan seems happier than I've seen him in weeks," Matilda said.

"I suppose Aus had to like one of us."

"I think *like* is a bit strong. Artan tells me he's still getting put through his paces whenever they go out."

"But he's enjoying it?"

Matilda shrugged. "He seems to be."

"Have you seen Hawk lately?"

Matilda shook her head. "He took that rejection hard."

"You think he's okay?"

"I hope so. Maybe he's off with Dianna somewhere. Keeping his head down until we leave. I didn't think it was possible, but he seems to want to leave this place more than we do."

William exhaled hard, his cheeks puffing. "It won't be easy when we go, will it?"

Matilda held the back of his hand. "We'll find a way. I think Max getting himself together will be the bigger challenge."

"And how long do we wait for that to happen? Gracie's right"—the red-headed girl sat with her dad in reserved courtside seats—"he will make the chances of our success much higher, but if he can't face mixing with the people in this community to watch a game of sport, how will he face going outside Dout again?"

The lights turned off before Matilda replied, the darkness so complete it pushed against William's eyeballs.

Matilda squeezed the back of his hand harder, leaned close, and whispered, "What's going on?"

"I've no—"

"Ladies and gentlemen, boys and girls." An omnipotent announcer. "Will you please welcome your champions"—he dragged out the *F* of Freddie's name so it came out more like a hiss—"Ffffffffffreddie and Aaaaaaaaaaaaaustin."

The crowd cheered and clapped.

The hairs lifted on the back of William's arms. This

should have been him. The next protector arriving to put on a show.

Whoosh! The door to the arena opened. A spotlight shone on Freddie as he entered. When Aus ran in behind him, tracked by another spotlight, the crowd grew louder, stamping and whistling.

The shrill peeps cut into William, forcing his shoulders up to his ears.

Aus ran to the centre of the court, raised his right hand, and turned full circle.

∽

After several minutes of applause, the rest of the lights came on, and the crowd quietened.

The first time William had seen Aus smile, he positively glowed from the adoration. "Okay, okay. Thank you, everyone, for the support. It's much appreciated. Now, we have some newbies watching for the first time today. So, for their benefit, I want to explain the rules of rumble puck." He pulled a small wooden puck from his pocket and held it in the palm of his hand. He tossed it in the air and caught it while he spoke. "This is the puck. There's a net at either end of the court. The idea is to get the puck into the net. The first one to do it five times wins."

William leaned close to Matilda and spoke from the side of his mouth. "What about the rumble part?"

"You can't run with the puck," Aus said, "you can only pivot. Other than that, there are no rules."

While Aus had been addressing the crowd, Artan and Nick took up their positions in their half of the court.

Aus walked towards his dad and held the puck in his direction. "Will you do the honours?"

The crowd applauded the beaming Jan when he got to his

feet. He raised the puck, and they fell silent. "May the best team win." He turned his back on the court and threw the puck over his shoulder.

Artan caught it.

The *crack* of Aus slamming his forearm into Artan's nose whipped around the arena. William winced with the rest of the crowd.

Matilda got to her feet and pointed at Aus. Several people looked at her, and before she could say anything, William tugged her down. "This is the game, Tilly. Let them get on with it."

A loud buzzer sounded, the crowd cheered, and Nick helped Artan to his feet. The lower half of his face a mask of blood, Artan wiped it away with his sleeve.

"Let them get on with it?" Although she'd sat down, Matilda shook her head and chewed the inside of her mouth. "Aus said it was the first to five. If he hits Artan like that four more times, there won't be an Artan left."

"That was a sucker-punch," William said. "Artan knows what's coming on the next round."

Jan stood up again, puck in hand.

Matilda's bouncing leg rubbed against William's. Her jaw tight, she breathed through her nose.

Jan launched the puck over his shoulder. It spun as it sailed through the air. This time, Aus didn't even wait for Artan to catch it. He swept his legs from beneath him, kicked him in the head, and picked the puck up from where it had fallen on the wooden floor beside him.

Aus and Freddie passed the puck between them, avoiding Nick on their way up the pitch. They slammed it into the net for the second loud buzzer.

Her teeth bared, Matilda said, "I swear, I'm going to fuck him up."

"Let Artan fight his own battles."

Although Artan had gotten back to his feet, Nick raised a hand at Jan, who nodded in response.

Matilda shifted forwards and perched on the edge of her chair. "What are they doing now?"

Artan and Nick huddled together in conversation while Aus turned to the crowd. His grin stretched from one side of his wide head to the other. His deep laugh echoed through the hall. "I don't know what they're planning, but I wonder if it's about how gracefully they lose? Or how many teeth they'll have left at the end of this game."

The crowd laughed.

William clapped a hand on top of Matilda's shoulder, keeping her seated. "Let him get on with it."

"You don't have a brother. You don't know what it's like."

"I still care about Artan."

"Then you should let me go down ther—"

Jan, puck in hand, turned his back on the court again, and William's heart sank. What would three more of these points do to—

Crack! Artan blind-sided Aus with a hard right jab. He knocked him to the ground, caught the puck, and threw it at Nick as he passed Freddie.

The buzzer sounded when Nick scored. The crowd fell silent. Most of the crowd.

"Yes!" Matilda jumped to her feet and punched the air. "Go on, Artan and Nick! You can do it."

William waited for her to sit down again and leaned close. "I told you he'd be okay."

On the next point, the second Aus threw the puck up to his dad, Nick tackled him to the ground while Artan attacked Freddie with a kick to the chest. For the second time, Artan caught the puck. He threw it from the halfway line. It hit the back of the net. The buzzer sounded. Two-all.

Freddie passed the puck up to Jan next. This time,

both Nick and Artan ran at Aus. They neutralised their biggest threat before running at Freddie next, wrestling the puck from his grip and making their way back up the court, passing the puck to one another to the other end.

William nudged Matilda as the buzzer sounded. "See!"

"All right." She rolled her eyes.

The puck remained in the net while the four of them fought in the arena.

Aus and Freddie both dwarfed Artan, but his slim frame hid his strength, and more importantly, his stamina. While the others were gasping for breath, he had the lung capacity to keep going. Both Freddie and Aus down, Artan retrieved the puck, threw it to Jan, caught it when Jan threw it back, and scored again.

"Yeargh!" A beacon of incandescence, William couldn't tell where the blood on Aus' face ended and his fury began. One hot red glowing mess, he charged Artan, his teeth clenched, his veins standing out like ropes on his neck.

Artan dropped into a crouch. At the last moment, he dodged to the side, grabbed the back of Aus' shirt, and steered him so he slammed, head-first, into the wall surrounding the court.

The crowd collectively dragged in air through clenched teeth. Even William winced.

Meanwhile, Nick caught the puck, Freddie closing in on him.

Artan ran across the court, received Nick's pass, and sent the puck goal-wards.

Most of the crowd fell silent on the final buzzer. Most of them. William and Matilda got to their feet and clapped. Gracie did the same.

"Excuse me." Matilda made her way through the seats.

William followed in her wake.

Aus rested a hand against the wall he'd collided with to help himself stand.

By the time William and Matilda reached the court, Aus had made it to the centre and had the crowd's attention. "It looks like Freddie and I have met our match." He wiped his bleeding nose with the back of his hand. "Well done, Artan and Nick. You played well. Until next time."

The crowd only applauded after Aus had, as if he'd given them permission to celebrate.

∽

WILLIAM AND MATILDA waited until the place had mostly emptied before they approached Artan. William patted him on the back. "Well done! I thou—" He lost the air from his lungs when Aus tackled him around the waist and drove him into the arena's wall.

Wide eyes, gritted teeth, he sprayed him with spittle when he said, "You need to wind your fucking neck in."

William pushed him away. "What?"

"There's no need to rub our noses in it. Artan and Nick won. We get it! You—"

Crack! Matilda came from the right and blind-sided Aus with a blow to the side of his head. He let go of William and turned on her.

Matilda landed a clean strike with a swift kick between his legs.

Aus gasped, grabbed his crotch, and fell to his knees.

About a quarter of the spectators remained in the hall.

"Have some fucking grace," Matilda said. She loomed over the downed Aus. "You lost, accept it. What kind of sport is it if you always win? In fact, from the way this crowd refused to celebrate Artan and Nick's victory, I'd question the validity of your legacy on this court. Have you heard the story of the emperor's new clothes?"

He opened his mouth, but for once he had no words.

Someone burst from the crowd. Jan might have been grey, his leathery skin showing his age, but he moved fast. He caught Hawk, lifted him in the air, and slammed him down, back-first, onto the hard floor. He leaned over him and jabbed a thick finger in his face. "Don't!"

"Hawk?" William said.

When Jan let go of the scarred hunter, Hawk stood up, shook his head and pointed at Aus. "You played that game like a fucking coward. You're a bully." He paused, recovering from where Jan had winded him. "Mark my words, you'll get yours." He shoved his way through the crowd as he exited the arena.

"Come on." Matilda reached out to Artan. "Let's get you cleaned up."

They followed the path made by Hawk. He'd now given them a choice. Did they back him and leave Dout? Leave Aus and his tyrannical rule? Move on like they wanted? Or did they wait for Max to get his head together and put Hawk in danger? How long would that take? And even if they waited, would he ever recover?

CHAPTER 14

"Will I ever get better?" Max said. He lay on his back in his room, staring up. He'd only been here a few days, but he'd spent so much time alone in this small pod, he'd learned every ornate twist and turn that made up the etching on the ceiling. He could draw the filigreed lines carved into the rough steel from memory.

Olga lay beside him. She turned her head so her warm temple rested against his. "Yes, you will!"

"But when? The others want to leave soon."

"And you don't have that in you right now?"

"No." He shook his head. "Nowhere near."

"Maybe it'll come. Like a switch turning on?"

It wouldn't just come. It might never come. "What do you think about staying here?"

Olga sighed and rolled her head away from his.

Whoosh! The door leading into the communal dorm opened. Their line of sight was blocked by their own closed door, but it didn't mute the throat-tearing scream. It ran to Max's core, adrenaline flooding his system.

Hawk screamed again, "I can't fucking believe it."

Max's thoughts slipped.

"The fucking audacity of that vile prick!"

Snarling diseased snapped through his mind.

"How fucking dare he do that?"

Cyrus' glazed eyes.

"Are you okay?"

The asylum.

"Max!" Olga had sat up and leaned over him. "Are you okay?"

His chest tight, Max fought to put his attention on her.

"Are you okay?"

His dry throat pinched when he swallowed. He nodded. He scratched his head. "Yeah, I-I think so."

Olga stood up. It gave Max the room to sit, his bare feet pressing against the cold steel floor. His head spun. Sweat lifted around his collar.

The raised voices in the communal area stopped making sense.

Something slammed against the dorm's wall. *Crash!*

Max yelped and folded over himself, leaning forward at the waist. He rocked and shook his head.

"Come on." Olga held her hand towards him. "Let's see what's going on out there. I'm sure it's not as bad as it sounds."

"Are you mad?" *Mad Max*. He shook his head. He pointed at the door leading to the empty room on the other side. "I think I should go that way. I can come back when things have calmed down."

"If you keep running away, you'll never be ready to move on."

Hadn't she been listening to him? Maybe he wouldn't ever be ready to leave this place. She needed to accept that.

But Olga tugged on his hand. "Come on!" She pulled Max to his feet and slapped the button beside their door.

Whoosh!

Even with Olga as a screen in front of him, the chaos in their communal room assaulted Max. Hawk paced back and forth. He threw a metal cup against the floor with a *crash!*

William and Matilda were tending to Artan, who sat on his bed, his face swollen and covered in blood.

One of Aus' crew stood in the corner with Gracie. William turned on her and threw his arms up. "What the fuck's wrong with him?"

Max halted. "I need to go back into my room."

But Olga pulled him forwards again. "I love you. You know that, right?"

"He's a prick," Gracie said. "I've told you that already."

Hawk kicked over his bedside table, and Max jumped.

Olga tugged on Max's hand again. "I said I love you. You know that, right?"

Max nodded.

"So trust me on this."

"You must have known what would happen," William said. "You didn't think to warn us?"

"You need to step outside your comfort zone." Olga stood directly in front of Max. "Otherwise, it will get so small you'll suffocate. You need to reconnect with the world, and this is a safe way to do it. These are your friends. They mean you no harm."

"Fucking piece of shit!" Hawk turned his bed over.

Max pulled away, but Olga held on. He needed to go back to his room. "What if I can't reconnect with the world?"

"You've already reconnected with me. We just need to do it one step at a time."

A lot of people needed him to be okay. He had to try for their sake. But his stomach knotted. Max shook his head and pulled back again.

Hawk threw his mattress across the room.

Olga stamped her foot and screamed, "Will you all shut the fuck up?"

The room fell silent. A single tone rang through Max's mind. A shrill and continuous note.

William clapped his hand to his mouth, his words muffled. "Oh, shit. Sorry, Max. I didn't see you there. I'm so sorry."

They all turned Max's way. The walls closed in. He tugged on his collar, but his throat still tightened.

Matilda spoke with a soft tone. "We're all a bit fired up, Max. Artan played a game of rumble puck with Aus and his mate Freddie. Artan and Nick were on the same team." The boy in the corner with Gracie raised his right hand as a greeting.

One of Artan's eyes had swollen shut. Dried blood coated his mouth and chin. "I'm guessing Aus and Freddie won?"

The face of a gargoyle, Artan laughed. "No. That was the problem. It all turned sour at the end."

Artan's swelling moved his features in unexpected ways. It itched Max's mind. The diseased were the same. Cheeks hung. Eyes bulged. Noses flapped. No face did what it should. "And …" He shook his head to get rid of the thoughts. "How has that affected relations in this place?"

Hawk stepped forwards. "They're f—"

"They're not that bad," Artan said. His eyes shot across the room to Gracie as if asking her permission. "I could still stay here longer."

"After what happened?" Hawk said.

"We all know Aus is a dick," Artan said. "No offence, Gracie."

She shrugged. "I've already said the same myself. Countless times. He's a weapons-grade knob-head."

"But," Artan said, "the rest of this place isn't bad."

"For someone who's been selected to go outside the

community, you mean?" Hawk shook his head. "It's all fucking rosey for you, isn't it? In case you hadn't noticed, things are a lot worse for me. I tried to attack Aus. I was unpopular before; how do you expect …" He stopped and rubbed his face with both hands. "You know what? It doesn't matter. I'm a big boy. I can handle myself. It's clear you fuckers don't have my back." His chest rose with his deep inhale. "Max, how are you feeling?"

How was he feeling? *Mad Max*. When would he be ready to move on? And if he didn't move on soon, would everything get worse when Gracie finally ratted him out for going outside and putting the community at risk? At least if he went now, he could get away before that bomb landed. "I … I, uh, I …"

Gracie stepped from the shadows and crossed the room towards them. Max had forgotten he and Olga were holding hands until she gripped so tight it hurt.

A warm smile on the red-headed girl's face. "You know what," Gracie said, "you do what you need to do. If you choose to stay"—she held eye contact with Max—"then that's fine with me. There will be no problems. You're safe here."

With every word Gracie said, Olga gripped tighter. At least Gracie had answered his question. She wouldn't rat him out. There had obviously been no repercussions from him going outside. A few days had passed. If there was going to be a reaction, surely it would have happened by now.

Everyone in the room watched Max. They wanted something from him, but what could he say? Force him to make a choice now, and he'd stay. No question about it.

"Come on." Olga pulled Max back towards their room. She hit the button to open the door, led him in, and closed the door behind them. "Look," she said, "I wanted you to be ready to leave with the others, but I can see that might not be the case. We need to get you feeling yourself again, but we can't rush it. My number one priority is staying with you, whatever else happens."

"Even if I never want to leave?"

Olga stepped so close to Max, her warm breath pushed against his face. She stared into his eyes and nodded. Every atom of Max's being pushed towards her. Half an inch separated their lips.

Olga kissed his cheek. She whispered in his ear, sending electricity down his spine. "Even if you never want to leave."

CHAPTER 15

Artan halted when Aus tugged on his empty bag. The straps pulled on his shoulders and lit up several of the sorest points on his body. They'd played rumble puck yesterday. His body needed a lot longer to recover. They'd come with larger bags for this trip than they'd had the last time they visited. Now they'd found a better way into their armoury, they needed to make the most of it and steal as much ammo as they could carry. How long would it take for the community to work out what they were doing?

"You should stay in Dout," Aus said.

"Huh?"

"What do you mean, *huh?*"

"You went at me like you wanted to kill me yesterday."

"That's how we play rumble puck. It doesn't mean I don't like you. I think you should stay. We could do with someone like you on our team. You might be young, but you have a lot to offer."

Slipping his spear sheath from his back, Artan rested it against the outside wall. The tips were coated with diseased blood. They encountered the creatures every time they went out. Hardly surprising with how many people they sent through the gates. Even in Dout, deep underground, when it quietened down at night-time, he heard the loud siren. It made his heart sink. More diseased coming through. And those who survived added to the enemy's number. Two communities hell-bent on eradicating people like him and his friends. But for what? What had they done to deserve such hatred?

Artan went first through the tight tunnel. At the other side, he shimmied along the back of the steel kennel and peered around it at the sleeping community. The cuboid buildings. The lights shining from each. The dogs were nowhere to be seen. Had they taken them out somewhere? But where? The siren hadn't sounded. What other use did they have? And when would they be back?

Artan jumped from the tap on his shoulder.

Nick smiled at him. "He's right, you know."

"Huh?"

"Aus. He's right. You should stay."

But how could he? Especially with how Aus had treated William. He'd been a brother to him for years. When he left, he'd be taking Matilda with him. He couldn't be separated from them. And things didn't look like they would change between William and Aus any time soon. Especially as he'd put them on guard duty that evening.

"Well?" Nick said.

If only he could stay. Artan shook his head. "It's not the time to be having this conversation. We've come here to get ammo."

The narrow steel ledge leading along the back of the kennel glistened with dew. A later hour than when they'd last visited. The best chance to make sure most of the community was asleep.

Artan made it halfway along the ledge when Nick hissed,

"I'm not giving up, you know. What will it take for me to get you to stay?"

He turned back. "Will you—" Artan's foot slipped. For the briefest second, he held his balance. Until he fell. "Oomph!" He landed on his left shoulder and clamped his jaw to suppress his scream. White-hot rods streaked from the point of impact all the way down his back. Nick stood above him on the ledge, his mouth hanging open.

A deep growl to Artan's right. He jumped up, his arm numb, his face sore from their game of rumble puck. He pulled his knife from the sheath on his hip. It shook as an extension of his trembling arm. He held it toward the dogs. "Stay the fuck back."

Fifteen dogs of varying shapes and sizes. There had been three times the number the last time they'd visited. Although, it still left him outnumbered by fifteen to one. A single stamp would break the backs of some, but it would take more than a knife to bring down the larger ones. Heads dipped, shoulders raised, they stalked forwards, the moonlight glinting off their bared teeth.

Crack! Nick landed beside Artan.

"What are you doing?"

Nick drew his knife and held it in the dogs' direction. "You're down here because of me. It's the least I could—"

The largest dog of the lot, jet-black and made from pure muscle, lunged forwards. Artan met its advance with a wild swing of his knife. He slashed the side of the creature's face, his stomach clamping from the deep cut. The dog yelped and withdrew. It didn't deserve to be attacked, but he needed to get out of there, and it gave him no choice.

His teeth clenched, Artan said, "That's clearly the alpha. If we scare the dominant ones, hopefully the rest will fall into line."

Another dog snarled and charged. Nick cut its left side, sending it back with a whimper.

Two charged Artan. He slashed one and kicked the lighter of the pair. His blow lifted the thing from the ground.

Shadows formed above them. Aus and the others.

"So what's the plan?" Nick said.

"I kinda hoped you'd tell me. You were the one who jumped down here."

Clop! Nick caught one dog's snapping jaws with a kick.

The dogs had formed a semicircle around them. They kept their distance, but they were still firmly in control of the situation.

Artan pointed at the gate on the other side of the pen. "That has to be the best way out. If it's anything like the doors in the rest of this place, it should open from the inside."

"Why don't we climb out?"

Artan's shoulder throbbed. He held it while shaking his head. "I can't."

"Shit! Sorry."

Artan lunged towards the next attacking dog, and Nick did the same beside him. Both beasts whined and withdrew to a safe distance.

Nick pointed. "Let's get them in there first." They'd divided the pen into two sections, the larger area for exercise, and a smaller space where the kennels were. "If we can lock them in their kennels, we can get out of here."

A deep bass note of hostility. Growling dogs. Raised hackles. Each of them wore their own unique stripe of aggression.

"If we don't do something fast," Nick said, "we're screwed."

"Fine," Artan said. "On three. One … two …"

Nick led the charge. He waved his arms and kicked out at the dogs, keeping his noise down.

Some dogs ran back and headed straight for their kennels. But the more brazen of the pack charged, including the alpha.

Artan and Nick versus six of them. The alpha's maw dripped blood from Artan's previous attack. He went for the muscly beast again and caught it clean, kicking it so hard it knocked the thick dog onto its back. It scrambled upright and retreated after the others, its tail between its legs.

Nick chased the remaining few in, kicking one dog in the ribs when it turned on him. "Close the gate behind me."

"What?" Artan said.

"Just do it!"

The opaque gate stood about eight feet tall. The hinges groaned when Artan pulled it shut with a *click!*

It shook. Nick must be climbing it from the other side. How would he know if Nick needed help?

But Nick's leg swung over the top, the bottom of his trousers shredded. He pulled the rest of himself over and fell, hitting the hard ground much like Artan had. The dogs' growls and snarls turned into yips and barks. Some of them howled.

Artan leaned over him. "Are you okay?"

At first, Nick winced and panted. He then smiled, which turned into a laugh.

"You're a mad bastard, you know that?" Artan shook his head and helped Nick stand. "Now let's get the hell out of here before those dogs wake up the entire community."

Artan led the way on wobbly legs. He'd taken too many beatings over the past few days. He shoulder-barged the gate open. The heavy contact tweaked every ache in his body. He stood aside to let Nick out first before closing the gate. He paused. It had a handle on the outside. The first one he'd seen in this place. A bar about an inch in diameter and about eight inches long. It sat in an irregular spot. A foot in from the edge. Not the most practical design. He grabbed the handle and twisted. It shifted, but only slightly. Another hard twist and it came free in his hand.

Aus joined Nick and Artan. He threw his arms up. "What the fuck was that about?" Thick lines dominated his heavy brow. "Are you trying to give us away? You know, I take back what I said about you joining us. You're a fucking liability." He pointed at the handle. "And what the fuck's that?"

"Just lead us to the armoury so we can stock up and get out of here," Artan said.

"You want to watch your tongue, boy." But despite the warning, Aus led them away.

An already familiar route, Aus guided them past cuboid houses, beneath barred windows, and even halted when they had wider areas to pass to make sure they had a clear run.

They closed in on the armoury. Aus sneered at Artan's limp. "What good are you to us in this state?"

"Half of my injuries are down to you, remember?" Artan held the handle he'd brought with him to the armoury's door. It connected with a magnetic *clunk!* A quick test tug before he yanked it harder.

Aus gasped when the armoury door popped open. His jaw hung loose, and he half laughed before leading the others inside, pulling his bag from his shoulder as he went.

Nick had moved to the back of the line. He paused by Artan at the open door. "Wow! You're smart. Another reason we need you running with us."

Artan twisted the handle free and gave it to Nick. "You take it. I'm sure there are more in this place if this is how they open the doors, but until you find them, you'll need it."

"Why me? Why don't you hold onto it?"

"Come on, Nick, you and I both know I won't be here

long. I might be welcome, but William is like a brother to me, and Matilda—"

"Is your sister." Nick sighed, took the handle from Artan, lowered his head, and dragged his feet as he walked into the armoury.

It tore at Artan's heart, but what could he do? He'd found something approaching happiness for the first time in what felt like years, but it wouldn't be complete if he couldn't share it with his sister. No matter what happened, she came first.

CHAPTER 16

"Fuck Aus. He's a fucking prick." William let go of the button on his walkie-talkie. The echo of his sentiment not only rang around the steel corridor, but through his mind from where he'd said it so many times in this place.

His walkie-talkie hissed when Matilda came back to him. "You don't think we should have this conversation somewhere more private?"

William peered through the window in the reinforced steel door. Another long view down another grey and empty tunnel. He said, "Move on!"

Matilda confirmed she also saw nothing. "Move on."

William walked to the next of the eight doors. Matilda, while he couldn't see her, checked the doors opposite his. They moved on a rotation with a clockwork tedium. Who knew how long they'd already been at it, but they had to go until morning. "I don't care who hears. Fuck him. It's nothing I wouldn't say to his face, and it's not like he hides his disdain for us. Artan's the only one he likes."

Despite hearing the white-noise hiss hundreds of times already that evening, the aggressive burst of static still cut through William. "And even then," Matilda said, "he was more than happy to beat the shit out of him when they played rumble puck."

"He's a snake. The sooner we get away from him and this place, the better." William reached the next door and pressed his nose to the cold glass. His breath turned to condensation. "We might not have a way of getting past the wall, but we'll work it out. Even if Max doesn't come with us."

"Maybe we could go under it?"

"You reckon?"

"There's no point in ruling it out before we've given it some serious consideration."

"Move on," William said.

A static wash followed by Matilda's tired voice. "Move on."

Eight doors. Each one identical. William drew a smiley face in the condensation on the next pane. He gave it crosses for eyes before wiping it away with his sleeve and peering down the long, bland corridor. He pressed the button on the side of his walkie-talkie. "You know, it wouldn't take much to convince me I've spent the entire evening peering down the same corridor."

Matilda came back to him. "The same steel walls."

"The same dull lights."

She laughed. "The same nothingness stretching away. Bland, grey nothingness."

"Feels like a metaphor for our time in this place. Walking in circles in the hope we'll end up doing something more than staring into the void. But you know what, no matter how we conform, and how hard we search for something other than an empty grey corridor—"

"That's all there is," Matilda said. "The definition of stupidity. Move on."

William snorted an ironic laugh. "Move on."

"So," Matilda said, "when do we leave this place? You told Max—"

"I know, and I feel awful. But as much as I want him to take as long as he needs, how much time is too much? What if he's never ready? He might be able to help us get through the wall, but if he never wants to leave, what then? We have to make the decision that's right for us too."

"It'll break Olga's heart."

"*If* she comes with us," William said.

"Are you saying we leave her as well?"

"Do you think this place is our home? We have to move on. But, were I in Olga's shoes and if someone asked me to choose between you and moving on, I'd choose you every single time."

William's eyes burned from his lack of sleep and searching in the poor light. "Move on."

He stared at the walkie-talkie. "Tilly?"

Seven knocks hit the other side of a door. A door close to Matilda.

William pressed the button on his walkie-talkie again. "Everything okay, Tilly? Tilly?"

They'd asked them to stay on their post. To always remain on opposite sides to one another. But fuck what they'd asked. William jogged around to Tilly, the hard-walled corridor amplifying his steps.

Whoosh! Matilda jumped aside as Aus stormed in, the rest of his crew on his tail. He jabbed a thick finger at his temple. "What took you so long, girl? Are you slow in the head? Can't you see how much I'm carrying? You have one fucking job. Let me in when I knock and be prompt about it. Jeez, what's wrong with you?"

"I'm sorry!" Matilda said.

Sweat lifted around William's collar. He tugged on his

shirt and drew calming breaths. He stood aside to let Nick and Aus past.

"Sorry's not good enough."

"Sorry's too fucking much," William said. "There's only two of us, you prick. If you knock at a door we're not right beside, you might have to wait a few seconds for someone to answer. You need to pull your head out of your arse."

"Who are you to talk to me like that? I've risked my life by going outside tonight—"

"Everyone risks their lives by going outside. Artan went with you. What, you want a fucking medal for that?"

"William," Matilda said.

"Yes, William. Listen to her."

William stepped closer to Aus. "I don't know who you think you are—"

"I'm someone you need to learn to respect, *boy*. In this place, I outrank you. You *will* pay attention to that. I don't know what you learned about etiquette before you came here, but my guess is your parents failed to teach you the basics."

William punched Aus. He caught him square on the nose. The broad man's eyes watered, but before he could retaliate, William shot backwards. Artan and Nick had grabbed one of his arms each. The other seven in their team restrained Aus.

Blood ran from Aus' nose. "That sucker-punch is the only way you're getting one over on me, *boy!* Come at me for a square go and see how you fare."

William sprayed spittle when he spoke. "I don't care about a fair fight. Talk about my parents again and I'll cut your throat in your sleep."

"What do you expect? You're a weasel. You're clearly the product of bad parenting."

William turned with a sharp twist and broke away from Artan's and Nick's grip.

Aus writhed against the restraint from the rest of his crew.

Crack! William punched him on the nose for a second time.

"Yeargh!" Aus shook, all seven of his crew fighting to hold him back.

Nick passed William on one side on his way to help contain Aus. Artan passed him on the other and shook his head. "I need to see if I can sort this out now."

"Someone had to stick up for your sister!"

"Well"—Matilda raised her voice over the chaos of the army of men dragging Aus away—"if we were welcome here, I'd say that's just changed things." She nodded up the hallway to see Jan walking towards them. "Uh-oh."

Red faced, a vein raised on his brow. The familial resemblance to Aus stronger than ever. "What's going on?"

"Your *son* crossed the line," William said.

"What did he do?"

"He forgot his manners." William stepped forwards.

Jan raised an eyebrow. Did William really want to pick a fight with everyone in the place?

"He thought he could talk to us like we're worthless," William said. "He spoke to Matilda like she was less than worthless."

"So your response was to attack him?"

"And I'd do it again in a heartbeat. He needs to learn respect."

"He's not the only one. Jeez," Jan said, "do you not know how to talk things out?"

"Not with an arsehole like your son, no."

Another set of steps ran around the corner.

"Gracie," Jan said, "you need to get a handle on your friends. At some point, they will have exhausted our hospitality."

"And you need to rein in your brother," William said.

Jan shook his head and walked away.

Gracie exhaled hard.

Jan's footsteps vanished into the distance, and Gracie looked from William to Matilda. William scratched his head and dropped his attention to the steel floor. "I'm sorry. I'd had enough before Aus returned. And then he was rude to Matilda and started making comments about my mum and dad." A crack in his voice. "I won't take that from anyone."

"What is it with you lot?" Gracie rubbed her face with both hands, her skin flushed when she pulled them back down. "I feel like I'm spending my entire time covering up your mess."

"What do you mean? Aus was being an arsehole, and we reacted. What other mess are you talking about?"

"You know what"—Gracie showed William her palm—"forget about it."

"I just want to say"—Matilda turned to William—"what you did then was okay by me." She reached across and rubbed his back. "He deserved it."

"How do you expect—"

"I'll stop you there, Gracie," William said. "First, you've been wonderful, and thank you for all you've done. Your brother, on the other hand, is a buffoon. We've had enough." He handed his walkie-talkie to her. "We're leaving tomorrow. I'm going to bed."

Gracie's lips tightened when Matilda also handed over her walkie-talkie. Both radios in her hands, she said, "Okay."

When they'd rounded the bend, William said, "You think Hawk will come with us?"

Matilda shrugged. "I can't see why not. He's keener than we are to leave this place."

"And Dianna?"

"Who knows?"

"And who cares?"

"Maybe a bit harsh."

"But fair."

Matilda nodded. "Yeah."

"Thank you," William said.

"For what?"

"For having my back. For being ready to move on. It feels like a weight off. I've had more than enough of this place already."

Matilda said, "It's cool. Now we have to see which of the others are up for it."

CHAPTER 17

Max woke, his heart beating in his throat. He chased his breaths to catch up and overtake his panic. Sweat covered his body from head to toe. He threw the covers aside, the cool air in his steel room lifting goosebumps on his flesh.

Olga stirred beside him and lifted herself up onto one arm. She peered at him through half-closed eyes and swept her dishevelled hair back. She croaked, "What's up?"

As his adrenaline died, Max settled and shook his head. He pulled the covers back over himself. "You know what? Nothing." He smiled. "I woke in a panic, because that's what I've been doing lately, but nothing's up. I slept a whole night with no nightmares. I feel …"

"Rested?"

He smiled again. "Yeah. For the first time in weeks. Since national service. Thank you."

Olga raised an eyebrow. "What are you thanking me for?"

"For standing beside me."

"Lying beside you, you mean?"

"Right." He rested a hand on her side. "Your support has really helped. Thank you."

"You don't need to thank me. Were the roles reversed …"

"But"—Max withdrew his hand and spoke to the mattress between them—"I still can't give you what most people would be able to. Being with me will always be lesser than."

"Wh—"

"I just want to say that if this becomes too much for you or, rather, too little, then I totally understand. You don't have to feel bad. You've tried. I can see that."

"Are you soft in the head? How many times will you try to push me away before you realise you're wasting your time?"

"I just … I want to let you know I understand. It's a lot to ask."

Half of Olga's mouth lifted in a smirk. "I'm tempted to kiss you now just to shut you up."

"By turning into a diseased in front of me?"

"Maybe I won't."

Olga leaned so close her hot breath pushed against Max's skin. Every hair on his body stood on end. Her proximity drove an electric current through his veins. Would she really kiss him? "Come on, Olga. Don't do this to me."

After she'd planted a lingering kiss on his forehead, she said, "Stop being soft, then. It's hard to be in a relationship with someone who keeps reminding you where the exit is. Just allow it to be, yeah?"

Someone knocked on the door. Max rolled out of bed, the steel floor frigid against his bare feet. He slapped his palm against the button, and the door opened with a *whoosh!*

"I'm sorry to bother you," William said before standing aside to show Matilda, Artan, and Gracie were all with him. "But we want to have a chat." His eyes flitted around the room, landing everywhere but on the semi-naked Olga. "I'll wait out here." He turned his back on them.

After putting on some socks, his boots, and a jumper, Max waited for Olga to get dressed before they both entered the dorm.

Artan always wore a scowl, as if lost in thought. But Gracie, Matilda, and William were all equally grave. A rock plummeted through Max's stomach. "What's going on?"

Whoosh! Hawk entered through the main door. His shoulders raised to his ears, he walked with a stoop and levelled a lingering glare on Artan.

"Where have you been?" William said.

Hawk paused, as if considering whether he should answer. "I've needed time to clear my head. Where's Dianna?"

"You don't know?"

"Why would I know? She's been aloof since we got here."

"William, can you just get on with it?" Olga said. "What do you want to tell us?"

"Max …" William said. "I told you to take as long as you needed to get your head together. That we'd wait for you."

"But that's changed?" Max said.

William winced. "Well … uh—"

"Yes, that's changed," Olga said. "Just fucking say it, William. It's much easier if you talk straight. You owe us that, at least."

"Okay," William said. "*I* need to move on." He held Matilda's hand. "*We* need to move on. Gracie's been a wonderful host."

"To some of you," Olga said. "I'm still trying to ascertain if she's going after my boyfriend or not."

Heat spread across Max's face. He cleared his throat. "Not now, Olga."

William turned to Gracie for a response. She shook her head. "But Aus is a weapons-grade psychopath," William said. "He's made it perfectly clear that we're not welcome."

"That's not true," Gracie said. "You *are* welcome. I'm sorry about my brother—"

William silenced her by raising his hand. "It's fine, honestly. Even if Aus is just one man, he's a big part of this community. He's one man who needs to give his approval for someone to remain here."

"Let me talk to Dad to see if he'll have a word. He listens to Dad."

"Maybe Jan could help?" Max said. He needed longer. He needed the time William had promised him.

"Thank you, Gracie." Matilda stepped towards the girl. "But we've made up our minds. Things will only get worse if we stay."

The same slamming pulse he'd woken with that morning tightened Max's chest. The walls closed in. If he went outside again now, who knows what will happen.

"Max," Gracie said.

The attention of the room turned on him. His already rapid pulse quickened.

"I understand your struggles. And if you want to stay here, you can."

"I *bet* you want him to stay," Olga said.

"You too, Olga. I assumed you wouldn't abandon him."

"But you hoped I might, eh?"

The heads of the others went between Olga and Gracie, following their exchange. "Olga," Max said, "this isn't the time or place." And then to Gracie. "Thank you for your kind offer. It means a lot." But William and the others had to go, and he had to go with them. Regardless of the consequences. How could he be the reason the group split up? He'd already taken the chance at a real relationship away from Olga. He couldn't take her friends from her too. Besides, what would life be like without them? They'd been through so much together. This day had to come, no matter how much time he took. And he'd woken up feeling better today than he had in weeks. Maybe this was as good as it got. "W-w-when are you thinking of leaving?"

William's reply reached into Max's stomach and tore it out. "Today."

Silence fell on the room. Artan shook his head. The brightened lights that signalled a new day caught the glistening rage in Olga's gaze.

"Okay." Max nodded. "I'm coming with you."

Olga gasped.

"I can face whatever's out there. I'm ready for this."

Artan's scowl deepened. His eyes turned from dark brown to black.

Hawk leaned in Artan's direction and winked at him. "Looks like you won't be able to run with Aus' crew anymore."

Artan worked his thick jaw. An involuntary movement to help him contain whatever simmered inside.

After throwing a glare in Hawk's direction, William stepped closer to Artan. "Do—"

"Don't!" His reply went off like an explosion. He stepped back with his hands raised, putting distance between him and William. "When are we leaving?"

"In about an hour," William said.

"I'll be ready. See you back here then."

Crack! The wall shook when Artan hit the button beside the door. He left, the door closing behind him.

"No." Olga shook her head.

"No?" William said.

"Max." Olga reached out and held both of his hands. "You can't go. I get why you want to, and I appreciate it, I really do, but this won't work out well for you. You're sacrificing yourself for the sake of the group ... again. When will that stop? You're unique and a valuable asset, but you're not ready to help us in those ways again. I wish you were, of course I do, but that doesn't make it true. For me to let you leave here today would be selfish."

Even while Olga spoke, the faces stirred in the shadows of Max's mind. Look over either shoulder and he'd come face to face with the snarling horror. No matter how strong he felt in that moment, they were waiting for him to fall. "Th—" The lump in his throat cut him off. He coughed to clear it. "Then you should go without me. I don't want to be the reason you're separated from everyone."

"Will you stop trying to make my decisions for me?" Tears swelled in her eyes, and she spoke through clenched teeth. "I'm wilful enough to make my own fucking choices. I *want* to be with you. Wherever you are. But I need you to stop pushing me away."

His own eyes burning, Max rubbed his face.

"Okay?" Olga said.

Max bit his quivering bottom lip.

"I'm sure you two," Olga said to William and Matilda, "understand more than anyone. I want to be with Max, so we have to make decisions for the good of our combined well-being."

William cleared his throat and nodded.

Matilda threw a hug around Olga and spoke in a broken whisper, her face buckling. "We understand."

While Olga and Matilda clung to one another, Max released a long and hard sigh. He might have slept well for the first time in weeks, but he hadn't slept well enough to face what waited for them outside. Not yet.

CHAPTER 18

Artan sat in the room's corner, his head in his hands. The first time he'd been in the pleasure dome alone. The first time he'd been able to choose his surroundings. A snowy mountaintop, the clouds below him. Had they dropped the temperature of the room for effect? Cold to his bones. To his heart. He stared at the floor, his entire being throbbing with a numbing buzz. But he had no choice over when he moved on. He couldn't be separated from his sister.

"Hey!" Nick entered the room. "I've been looking for you!"

"Well, I'm here."

Nick's shoulders sagged. His smile faltered. "Are you ... okay?"

"What do you want, Nick?"

"I ... uh, I didn't *want* anything. Other than to see how you're doing."

Snow swirled around them. Puffs of white dust blew from the jagged tips of rock. Nick hovered in the doorway. "What?" Artan said. "You want a fucking treat or something? You were looking for me; you've found me; what now?"

Nick wrapped his arms around himself. His eyes steeled. He turned as cold as the exposed rock in their imaginary environment. "Do you want to tell me what's going on?"

"Why does there have to be something going on? Why can't I just want a bit of space?" He tugged at his clothes as if they were too tight. "This place is making me claustrophobic. *You're* making me claustrophobic."

The steel left Nick's brown eyes. He rested a palm against his chest. His throat bobbed. "I ... I'll go, then."

The words didn't belong to Artan. They were being spoken by a dark destructive force deep within him. "You do that."

Nick left the room.

CHAPTER 19

William tested the weight of the sword in his hand, slid it into the sheath across his back, and hugged Gracie. "Thank you." The ladder out of there was embedded in the wall. A thirty-foot climb to the hatch at the top.

"You're welcome." She stepped back and stood next to her dad, who'd come with her, Max, and Olga to see them off. "I just wish I could have done more for you. Like, make my brother be less of a dick."

"I think if you had any power over that, you would have made him less of a dick years ago."

Gracie laughed. "He came out of the womb with a chip on his shoulder."

Jan cleared his throat and looked away. They'd said enough.

William stood close by while Matilda and Olga clung onto one another. When they parted, Olga pointed at them and spoke through a clenched jaw. "Make sure you find a way past that fucking wall and get yourselves the life you're chasing, okay?"

A lump in his throat, William hugged Olga and then

moved on to Max. "Thanks for everything you've done for us, man. All of us owe you a thousand life debts."

"You can say that again," Gracie said.

Olga threw a scornful glare her way.

Gracie shrugged. "What?"

Before Olga could reply, William said, "No sign of Dianna?"

"She's been AWOL for a while now," Hawk said. "She's not wanted much to do with us since we've been here."

"Do you think she knows we're leaving?" William said.

Hawk shrugged. "I think the question is, do you think she cares?"

Although Artan moved down the line, hugging their friends one after the other, he did it in silence. Dark bags sat beneath his eyes, and he held his jaw in a tight clench.

Hawk followed Artan's lead. At the end of the line, he said, "I won't miss this place one bit, but I'll miss you all. We've been through a lot."

"Artan," Jan said, "I wanted to thank you for working out a way to bolster our ammo supplies. It'll make a big difference should we ever need to defend ourselves. It's a shame Aus and the boys won't have you running with them anymore."

"I feel that too," Artan said. He clamped his jaw even tighter, as if fighting against a need to say more. His dark eyes dropped to the floor.

The tock of Gracie's feet against the steel ladder, she went up first and freed the lock on the hatch with a *clunk*. Daylight flooded in. The glare burned William's already itching eyes. He rubbed his face and remained focused on their exit. They'd said their goodbyes. They had to go now before they changed their minds. Before they lost their nerve.

The cold steel rungs were rough with rust. His sword sheathed on his back, he climbed out of the exit into a new day. A new start. When Matilda came out next, he waited for her to climb free before he took her hand. "We will get past that wall."

She offered him a tight-lipped smile.

Hawk and Artan followed them out. They all shared one last hug with Gracie before she climbed back into the hole and closed the hatch behind her. It became a part of the scenery. They were back amongst the ruins of the old church, the skeleton of an old building built in homage to a now long-forgotten religion.

"So what are we waiting for?" Matilda said. Artan and Hawk had already walked away.

William stared at the space where the hatch had been. "I'm not sure."

"You thought we might have found a reason to stay?" Matilda said. "That Aus might have suddenly seen the value we brought to the community and would have changed his personality?" She snorted a laugh. "Not much chance of that happening." She took William's hand and led him after the others.

"I dunno what I was expecting. I suppose it all feels a bit—"

"Final?" Matilda said.

"Yeah. Another chapter's ended."

"We've had a lot happen in a very short space of time."

"Ain't that the truth," William said. "The first day of national service seems like a lifetime ago."

Her grip tightened. "It seems like several."

"And," William said, "now we face getting over the wall. I think it's going to be much harder with just four of us."

"Of course it will."

Hawk and Artan were about ten feet ahead of William and Matilda. They carried spears, raised and ready to use.

And they'd see plenty of action. Especially as they got closer to the wall.

"Has Artan said anything to you?" Matilda said.

"About what?"

"I dunno. Something's happened, but for the life of me I don't know what it is. I always thought I knew him well. We've always told each other everything."

"It's a big deal, leaving Dout behind. Especially with what lies ahead. Maybe he's just trying to prepare himself."

∾

THE WIND on the brow of the hill tossed the long grass. It burned William's already sore eyes. The beds in Dout might have been more comfortable than any he'd slept on in the past few weeks, but he'd not had a restful night while they stayed there. The wall stretched out in front of them. Impossibly tall. Impossibly wide. Impossibly sheer. William exhaled, his cheeks puffing. "There has to be a way to get over it. Even without Max."

"Although, before we think too much more about that ..." Hawk had turned his back on the wall and faced the way they came. He squinted against the sun's glare and pointed down to their right.

"Shit!" William said. A small army of about one hundred and fifty soldiers. They marched with an equidistant space between each person, forming a perfect square of military might and order.

"And look there." Matilda pointed this time. Down to their left. Maybe fifty men. Less organised, but as clear in their intent. "Is that the community we took the solar panels from?"

"Maybe," William said. "There's been no siren to call them to the wall. Where do you think they're going?"

Artan tutted. "I'd say it's pretty fucking obvious. We need to get back and warn them. We need to fight beside them."

"But they locked the door after we left," Hawk said. "You saw what happened to that man in Aus' crew when he came back on his own. And they *liked* him. There's no chance they're letting us back in."

"We have to try," Artan said. "If they know they're coming, they'll be able to stop them, but if this lot catches them by surprise …"

"Lambs to the slaughter," William said.

Hawk said, "How do you know they've discovered Dout?"

"Honestly?" Artan said. "I don't. But we have friends back there, and if there's any chance they're going to get attacked, we have to warn them."

Matilda raised her eyebrows at William. "We owe Max and Olga at the very least."

"You agree with Artan?"

Matilda shrugged.

"We have to vote on it," William said. "Who says we go back?"

Artan's hand shot up. Matilda's a second later. Hawk kept his by his side.

"Even if you decide to move on," Artan said, "I'm going back. Vote or not."

William raised his hand. "Regardless of what we think of Aus, our friends are down there. Our friends and a lot of innocent people."

"It's fucking suicide," Hawk said. "And we don't even know if they've discovered Dout."

Matilda pointed at the two groups of people. "Unless we're certain of where those two armies are heading, we have to play it safe."

Hawk pouted and folded his arms across his chest. "I

reckon you've looked at this wall and are glad of the excuse to leave it for another day."

"Come on," Artan said, leading them back down the hill. "The sooner we get back, the more time there will be to prepare for whatever's descending on Dout."

CHAPTER 20

Max walked behind Gracie with Olga behind him. Best to keep them apart. They'd chosen to remain in Dout, so they needed to keep the drama to a minimum. They entered the surveillance room, Jan and Aus already waiting for them inside.

"So," Gracie said, her dad and brother watching on, one side of them lit up from the glowing wall of screens. Jan wore the soft warmth of kind acceptance. Aus scowled, his thick brow pressing down over his eyes. Gracie held his glare for a few seconds before she continued, "This is one job we need to do twenty-four hours a day." She showed Max and Olga the screens with a sweep of her arm. "This is our early warning for any trouble."

"If you see an enemy on the screen," Max said, "how long do you have to react?"

"We've never faced that scenario," Gracie said. "But they'd have to open a locked hatch, get down the ladders, and get along the corridors. I dunno." She shrugged. "Half an hour?"

"What do you know?" Aus leaned against the far wall opposite the door. Far enough from the group to not be a part of the conversation, but close enough to interject whenever he damn well pleased. "You just pulled that number out of your arse."

"Give me a better guess, then," Gracie said.

"Why would I put a time on something we can't possibly predict? Bottom line," Aus said, "we see trouble, we need to react fast. We need to get ready for war. And that includes you." He kicked off from the wall and marched over to Max. "So far, you've opted out. If we ever get to a point where we truly need you, you'd best show up. If you don't, I'll cut your throat myself."

Max stepped back a pace. "I …"

"What?" Aus tilted his head to one side. "You'll what?"

Heat smothered Max's face. He dropped his focus to Aus' thick leather boots.

"Like I thought."

Maybe they should have left with the others. But they'd made their choice now. A choice where Max's cowardice had separated Olga from her friends. And now he couldn't ever tell her he'd made a mistake. Besides, they knew what they were getting with Aus. Even his own sister hated him. They couldn't let Aus' problem become their problem.

"And just so you know," Aus said, "it wasn't my choice to let you remain here."

Olga flashed him a facetious smile. "You've already made that abundantly clear."

Aus said, "I know, but I feel it needs spelling out for the more mentally challenged." He nodded at Max.

"Aus!" Jan said. The boom of his voice whipped around the room. "That's quite enough."

"So, hopefully," Gracie said, flipping her brother the bird, "you've now seen Aus doesn't run this place. He needs reminding from time to time. He has a lot of opinions, and a lot of them are utter bullshit."

Wrinkles spread from the edges of Aus' tightened lips. "These two might be scared to tell you how it is, but I'm not. You and your friends have been nothing but a liability since you got here. You've taken more than you've contributed"—he pointed at Max—"you especially. Artan was the only one who offered anything meaningful."

"Wait a minute." Gracie walked over to the wall of screens and leaned close to one. "They've come back."

Max's heart lifted. "They've changed their minds?" He smiled at Olga, who continued to glare at Aus.

"They'd best not think they're coming back inside," Aus said. The group closed in on the camera, Artan leading them. "One," Aus counted on his fingers, "don't get caught or seen. Two, if you get caught or seen, don't come back here. Three, if you come back here and someone's following you, don't try to get … oh, fuck!"

William waved both his hands above his head.

"Why doesn't he plant a fucking flag where the hatch is?" Aus said. "You see!" A raised vein streaked his brow, and his face turned puce. "They're a fucking liability."

"What if they've come back to warn you about something?" Max said.

"I'd rather they didn't bother. They've been followed, I can guarantee you."

"No you can't," Olga said. "You've got no clue why they're back. Stop being such a know-it-all prick."

Aus closed the distance between him and Olga. Twice her size, the thickset man loomed over her. Max glanced at the doors along one wall. Weapons behind every one of them.

"Ho!" Aus said. "Are you seeing this, Gracie?" He pointed at Max. "Did you just catch your boy looking at the armoury?" He smiled and shoved Olga aside. His hot breath pressed against Max's face. "But we both know he doesn't have the stones. This life has castrated him."

Max balled his hands into fists.

"Stare at me like a moody little brat all you want. If you're not going to do anything, you need to sit the fuck down."

"Someone will cut your throat one of these days," Olga said.

Jan stepped between Aus and Olga. "The question is, what are they doing? What do they want? They're asking for something."

"If they've been followed ..." Aus said.

"They know the rules," Max said. Aus raised an eyebrow at him, but Max held his ground. "Despite what you think of them, we know them better than you, and we know they wouldn't risk all the people in this place by leading danger here. They've come back for a good reason."

"Then we have a dilemma," Jan said.

"No." Aus shook his head. "We don't. We need to leave them out there."

"Are you deaf?" Max said. "They've come back for a reason. I'm telling you."

"And why should we listen to you?"

"Gracie," Max said, "because your brother's too dumb to listen."

"*What?!*"

But Max kept his attention on Gracie. "I'm appealing to your greater intelligence. We have to go to them. Let them back in. They've come back here for a reason. We ignore that and we might end up regretting it."

"I still—"

"Will you shut the fuck up, Aus?" Max said.

"What?"

"You've been crystal clear in making your point, several times. Take the hint. No one gives a shit what you think. Now wind your fucking neck in."

"Are you threatening me?"

"Take it however you want. I don't care. But I'm telling you the reality of what's in front of you. I'm trying to help your community. Also, look at the screen, you dullard. Do you see them going anywhere? The only reason this place will get revealed is because you're too pig-headed to trust anyone's judgement but your own."

"You need to—"

"Do you see them going anywhere?" Max's voice echoed in the room. "Answer the fucking question."

Trembling with his restraint, Aus shook his head. "No. I don't."

"So you're going to put the entire community at risk by leaving them out there? The longer they wait, the more chance there is of them being seen."

"I ought to kick you out when we go down there."

"But it's not your choice, is it? Jan, are we going to do this?"

"Yes." Jan nodded. "I think you're right. Come on, let's go to them."

OF COURSE, Aus complained every step of the way, and of course, they all ignored him. They'd gotten what they needed. Screw Aus and his precious ego.

Their steps clicked against the steel floor in stereo. All five of them marched with metronomic synchronicity. Olga held Max's hand. He might not have stuck up for her in the moment, but he'd rediscovered his spine. Besides, if he tried to fight Olga's battles, no matter how much he'd wanted to, he'd be at war with her and whoever she'd confronted.

Gracie climbed the ladder leading to the hatch. *Clack!* She freed the lock and pushed it open.

"Thank the heavens!" Artan entered first. He followed

Gracie back down and jumped off at the bottom.

Aus grabbed the front of his shirt and slammed him against the wall. "What the fuck are you doing coming back here like that?"

Artan fought to prize Aus' hands off him.

Aus slammed him into the wall again. "What's fucking wrong with you?"

William landed in the tunnel next. His fists balled, he approached Aus. But before he could get close enough, Max punched Aus on the side of his head. *Crack!*

Jan jumped in and dragged Aus away. No questioning his alpha status, he tossed his son aside. The strong man, a boy in the face of his father's wrath. He cowered while Jan raised a halting palm at him. "Just stop, Aus. Let them speak."

"Thank you." Artan nodded at Jan. And then to Aus, he said, "We haven't given you away. We know the rules. We've come back to help. When we got to the top of the hill overlooking the wall, we saw two armies closing in. Now, it might be a coincidence. They might not be heading here, but they looked ready for war, and they were coming this way. They appear to know what they're looking for."

Max's arsehole clenched, and he damn near lost his bowels where he stood. Until that moment, he'd not allowed himself to put two and two together. "You really think they're coming here?"

"We'll find out soon enough. The larger of the two armies was heading this way." Artan pointed up. "Like they knew the location of that hatch. We got far enough ahead of them to get here safely and warn you."

Hawk and Matilda inside, the hatch above them closed. The hatch Max had come through the night Gracie saw him. But not just Gracie. Fire spread across his face, and he dropped his focus to the floor. Gracie's scrutiny burned into him. What had he done?

CHAPTER 21

"Surely they're going to attack soon?" Artan said. He kept his voice low, the hatch the army had stationed around at the top of the ladder. "They've been up there for hours."

Nick stood beside him, his Adam's apple protruding from where he stared up at the hatch.

"I can now see why Dout is buried so deep," Artan said. "There's no chance of someone digging into this place. And when they attack"—he pointed to where Nick already had his focus—"a lot of them will have to fall for them to get in here."

They'd set up their first line of defence behind the now partly closed doors a third of a mile away. The section they could close off and blow up should the need arise. In another situation, being so far from the enemy might have made things difficult, but the narrow tunnel would condense the soldiers into a small space. Shoot in their general direction and they'd hit something.

A walkie-talkie clipped to his hip, Artan had turned it off. If he needed to contact the others, he would. They couldn't afford for the static hiss to give away their location. The less their attackers knew, the better.

"When do you think they're going to come through?"

"Dunno." Nick shrugged.

"That's the first thing you've said in ages," Artan said.

"We need to keep quiet."

"We are." Artan had whispered the entire time.

"Besides, what good is it making baseless guesses? We don't know when they're going to attack. If we set an expectation by guessing, we might not be ready when it happens. Come on." Nick turned from Artan. "We need to check everything else is in place."

Artan remained close to the ladders while Nick walked away. When Nick didn't turn back, he ran after him.

Small cubes lined the tunnel where the walls met the ceiling. Enough explosives to bring the corridor down on the attacking army should their guns and bullets fail them.

"Why do they hate us so much?" Artan said.

"Huh?"

"Those soldiers back there. Why do they hate us?"

"We can only guess."

"Go on, then."

"I don't like guessing."

"Humour me."

"You think you've earned that?" Nick said.

Artan halted, but Nick continued walking. He ran for a second time to catch up with him.

"They're forced through the wall to die, right?" Nick said.

Artan shrugged.

"My guess, and as you know, I dislike the inaccuracies of guessing, but, gun to my head, I'd guess the people who force them through the wall sound like us. Also, we've been robbing them for years, have killed their people in retaliation for them killing ours, and Dout is a community worth taking by force …"

"You have the perfect cocktail of resentment and motivation."

"Exactly."

The partly closed doors were manually operated. They couldn't afford for a power cut to render them useless. Nick turned sideways to pass through the gap. Artan followed him a few seconds later.

They'd left a space in the doors wide enough to shoot through and wide enough to pass through when turning sideways. But they'd made it narrow enough to be a thick shield against an army's attack. Two guards on either side. Two men and two women. All four of them tight-lipped. Stoic. Contained. If they were anything like Artan in that moment, they had the pulse of a galloping horse. Each pair stood by a stack of guns. No two weapons were the same. Each one handmade. "And you're sure these guns will work?" Artan said.

"They work like they're supposed to," Nick said. "They might not look the part, but when you point them at what you want to kill and pull the trigger, they'll fulfil their purpose. And now we've done a few supply runs to their community, we have enough ammo to hold them off."

A wheel to manually operate the doors protruded from the left wall. It had a keyhole above it. A similar one on the other side. The keys were in, ready to turn. Nick inspected one and then the other.

"Two people have to turn these at the same time?" Artan said.

Nick nodded. "When we want to bring the tunnel down on top of them, yes."

The tunnel, like all the tunnels in Dout, had two sets of doors that when closed would divide them into three equal sections. Each section about a third of a mile long. The second set of doors, the set closer to Dout's main community, had also been partly closed, but they'd left them slightly wider to accommodate a hasty retreat. If they couldn't stop the army by shooting them as they descended the ladders, and then by collapsing the tunnel in on them, then they could come here. A similar pile of weapons on either side. Their last defence. "There's only a few hundred soldiers up there," Artan said, "so I'm not expecting us to be forced back this far, but surely if they get to this point, they'll be considerably weakened. The job here has to be cleaning up and repelling the few who remain."

"I hope you're right," Nick said, nodding at the next set of four guards, two on either side of the tunnel, as he passed them.

Nick slammed seven knocks against the last door. Locked, as always. The viewing window, made from thick glass like those in the other two doors, showed the guard's face. *Whoosh!* She let them in. The only door of the three they could operate both manually and electrically.

Artan had stared at Nick's back for most of their walk down the corridor. And the same happened on their way to the pleasure dome until Nick paused before entering. "Why didn't you tell me?"

"Really?" Artan said. "You want to have this conversation now?"

"You want me to save it? We might die today."

"I'm not planning on it. We've got this. That army's too small."

"That doesn't mean we're all walking away from this. And in case you hadn't worked it out, we're going to replace those guards by the doors and become the first line of defence." Nick slammed his hand against the button to enter the pleasure dome with a *crack!*

Whoosh. The door opened.

They'd told Artan and the others there were over two hundred and fifty people in Dout. Until now, it had been hard to believe. He'd passed it off as an exaggeration to keep the newest arrivals in check. But the packed pleasure dome pushed his cynicism aside. One hundred and fifty to two hundred people in there. Footage of an underwater scene played with calming music. For what good it did. The place smelled of sick and flatulence. Many pale faces. Many pairs of bloodshot eyes and tear-streaked cheeks. The children and the elderly made up a large percentage of the crowd. They hugged one another as if they didn't know who would look after whom. Their fear contagious. Just being in this room turned Artan's throat dry. His stomach churned.

If Nick felt it too, he hid it well. "We have everything under control." The acoustics of the high ceiling amplified his voice. "There's nothing to worry about. They're only a small army. We'll drive them back, and everything will be okay. You're all gathering here as a precaution." While he addressed the room, he made his way to the centre, cutting a path for Artan to follow.

A previously invisible hatch lay open. It revealed the escape tunnel.

"Uncle Nick?"

A small girl of about six years old slammed into Nick and wrapped her arms around his waist. He stroked the back of her head. She had long and straight blonde hair, pale skin, and blue eyes. Of all the people in the room, Artan would have picked her as the last person to call Nick uncle.

"Are we going to die, Uncle Nick?"

Silence rippled away from the girl. She spoke for everyone.

Although Nick shook his head, he took a moment. "Not if I have anything to do with it." He hunched down in front of her and held her hands. "I'll die before I let anything happen to you, okay?"

The girl nodded.

Nick led Artan back out of the room.

Artan gasped as if he'd been holding his breath. His lungs were tight, and he placed a hand over his hammering heart. "Jeez, I thought I was going to have a panic attack. If there was ever a good reason to fight …"

The sides of Nick's eyes tightened. The chink in his stoicism.

"You didn't tell me you were an uncle."

"This is a close community. Lots of the kids call me uncle."

Artan laughed. "I bet they don't call Aus uncle."

For the first time since Artan had returned to Dout, Nick smiled. His expression fell again, and he said, "Indulge me. Why didn't you tell me?"

"I'd already decided. I had to go. I won't be separated from Matilda."

"But you didn't give me a chance to decide. You didn't ask me if I wanted to come with you."

"How could I have asked you that?"

"You could, and should have. It's a claustrophobic life down here. I feel like I've been waiting for the right opportunity to leave."

"And a suicide mission over an impassable wall was that opportunity?"

Nick's words cracked when he said, "The opportunity was never a what, it was a who. At least respect me enough to ask me next time, okay?"

"I'm sorry," Artan said. His fingers twitched with the need to reach out. Instead, he balled his hands into fists. "I won't do it again."

"Thank you. And I'm glad you're back. I just wish the circumstances were different."

"Me too. We'll get through this."

"I hope so," Nick said. "I liked the look of my future."

∽

Back in the surveillance room, Gracie, Jan, Aus, Freddie, William, Hawk, Olga, and Max were all there. They fixed on the one screen that showed the army above.

Artan leaned close to get a better look. They'd built something in the background, but the night hid all but its silhouette. "What's that?"

"A barricade," Aus said. "To keep the diseased out while they attack us."

"I'd say this means they're going to attack soon," Gracie said. "They clearly know where the hatch is, but I'm guessing they don't realise we have cameras on them."

"Or they don't give a shit," Aus said.

Gracie shook her head. "There are too few of them to not give a shit. If they knew they didn't have the element of surprise on their side, I'm certain they wouldn't be attacking us."

"I think Gracie's right." Jan's deep voice cut through the room. His authoritative boom. He didn't speak often, but when he did, people listened. "They would have disabled those cameras if they knew they were there. There are ways to do it that would keep us guessing. They could block it with something that makes it look accidental, but hides what they're doing. There are too few of them for them to be confident they can take this place without it being a surprise attack."

"Are we going to speak about it?" Aus said.

Gracie shrugged. "Speak about what?"

"Someone's fucked up." Aus punched his left palm. It connected with a *crack!* "Someone's given away the location of this community."

Gracie said, "While I agree with you, Aus, I think someone *has* blown our cover, and we'll make them pay, but shouldn't we be preparing for the very real threat in front of us right now? It seems like the wrong time for a witch hunt. This is a winnable fight, but we need to make sure we're as prepared as we can be."

"Everyone's in the pleasure dome?" Jan said, cutting in before Aus could reply. How many times had he played referee over the years?

Nick nodded. "Yep, and the escape hatch is open."

"Right, let's get ready for this."

Gracie leaned close to the wall of screens. "Oh shit! Uh … Dad." The way she said it twisted tension through the room. It wound Artan's shoulders into his neck.

"I don't want to hear this, do I?" Jan said.

Gracie pointed at the screen, and Aus said it first. "Oh, fuck! That's why they made their barricaded area so large."

More soldiers streamed in through the barriers.

"That must be why they waited until night-time," Aus said. "That many people on the move would attract the attention of the diseased. Doing this in the dark is their best bet."

Jan sighed and rubbed his brow. "They must have known we were watching them. That we'd be confident we could fight them off. They knew we'd give them the time to set up their defences. Those first few hundred were the construction team." He squinted at the screen. "How many more do you think there are now?"

"Too many," Aus said. "Five hundred more? A thousand?"

"We're screwed," William said. "We need to get away from this place before it's too late. Shut the doors, blow the tunnels, and go through the escape hatch."

"The escape hatch is a last resort," Gracie said. "It's slow going. It'll take a while to get us all down it. Also, it emerges much closer to the wall, so even if we do all get through, there's a high chance of us bumping into a shitload of diseased at the end."

"You don't have a camera at its exit?" William said.

"No." Gracie shook her head. "The tunnel's over two miles long. We can't get a camera that far out."

"Wait!" The room turned their attention on Artan. "I have an idea." He pointed at the screen. "We have to assume they only know where one entrance is, right?"

"It looks that way," Jan said.

"I think we should go out through an exit on the opposite side. Use the darkness to our advantage, and attack them from the rear. Even if it's from long range and it's only a handful of us, we'll be able to cause enough chaos at a crucial time to throw the battle in our favour."

"Fish in a barrel," Jan said.

"Exactly. In that pen, they're an easy target. And they probably won't be able to fight back. They might have avoided the diseased on their way over, but the second they fight us, the noise will bring every one of those foetid bastards down on them. They look like they think they're in control. We need to use their confidence against them."

Jan held his chin in a pinch. After a few seconds, he said, "As far as ideas go, I think that's the best we have. Let's do it."

CHAPTER 22

The handmade gun was heavy in William's grip. Ugly and heavy. The straps of his rucksack tugged on his shoulders, filled with the ammo Artan helped steal from their neighbouring community. Ammo they intend to turn against its manufacturers to stifle their attack.

Olga walked ahead of them along the tunnel beside Rufus, one of the quieter members of Aus' crew. About five feet ten, broad shouldered, and in his early twenties, he had his hair shaved to the scalp. William tried to mimic how he held his weapon. He gripped it with both hands and pointed it at the wall on his left.

Artan and Nick led the way.

Matilda at his side, William spoke so only she heard. "You know, I reckon we're in a much better position than anyone else."

Her own ugly gun in her hands, Matilda cocked an eyebrow. "How so?"

He pointed at the ceiling. "It's dark up there, so we'll be hidden from sight. There's only a few of us, and we're going to spread out, so we'll be hard to spot."

"Six of us against an army is hardly stacking the odds in our favour."

"Six of us, each carrying a backpack filled with ammo. Also, they've penned themselves in. If we take the higher ground, we'll be able to take shots at them for fun, and they'll have no escape. And if shit goes south, we won't be underground with an army descending on us. Imagine what it's going to be like down here if we don't win this. At least we'll be able to run."

"You think Olga will leave Max?"

"No, and I'm not planning on leaving anyone either, but, you know, worst case …"

Matilda raised her gun. "Do you think these will work? They look far from reliable."

"Jan said we just need to point them and pull the trigger."

Artan arrived at the ladder first. Thirty feet of rungs leading to the escape hatch at the top.

Rufus switched off the walkie-talkie clipped to his right hip. They didn't need that thing giving them away while they snuck through the darkness.

William's heart galloped. His stomach clamped, and he drew a deep breath.

Matilda reached across to him. "We'll be okay."

"I—" William's dry throat robbed him of his reply. He nodded instead.

Clack!

William jumped.

Artan pushed the hatch open. The strong wind from outside ran down into the tunnel. William turned his face into the cool breeze. He closed his eyes and inhaled again. They had this. They could run whenever they needed.

After Artan climbed out, Nick followed him. Rufus and Olga went next, and William went ahead of Matilda.

The strong wind and poor light burned William's tired

eyes. It had already been a long day. The moon ran a highlight over the clumps of trees scattered throughout their environment. The long grass swayed. He stood aside for Matilda and forced a smile at her after she'd closed the hatch. They were all in now.

Matilda said, "At least it's quiet up he—"

"Artan!" William said, turning away from her.

Artan halted, threw his arms wide, and ran back over to William. "What?"

"You didn't see that?" William said.

"See what?"

"A flash of light."

"No." Artan shook his head. "Maybe it was the moon's reflection."

One hand raised to implore Artan to wait, William said, "Let's just hold on for a moment."

Another flash of light punched through the darkness. Several hundred feet from them and about fifty feet to the left of the first. And then another, even farther left, like all the lights were connected. Like they were talking to one another.

"Shit!" Olga said. "Get back inside now."

"We can't," Rufus said. "If we go back in there, we're going to show them where the entrance is."

"They just watched us climb out," William said. "I think they already know where it is."

A flash of light in the distance, accompanied by a *crack!* A bullet whooshed past.

A light as bright as the one in the sports hall shone on them. It came from the same direction as the small torches. It tracked their path, overtook them, and shone on the closed hatch.

"They clearly already know where the entrance is. The

best thing we can do is get back inside and lock them out." William ran to the hatch and pulled it open.

Olga climbed into the hole first. William let Matilda in next, and then Rufus. Both Artan and Nick returned fire, shooting blind.

William climbed backwards into the hole, his feet damp from the long grass and now slippery against the metal rungs.

The *thwip* of flying bullets cut through the air above them as Artan and then Nick climbed back into the community. Nick pulled the hatch shut. *Crash. Clack!* He secured it with the bolt.

William jumped from the ladder with a few feet to go and stepped aside to clear the way for Artan and then Nick. All of them panted. All of them stared at one another.

After unclipping the walkie-talkie from his belt, Rufus turned it on. The hiss of static crackled in the tunnel. He pressed the button. His voice wavered when he said, "Jan, we have a big fucking problem."

CHAPTER 23

What did Gracie mean when she told Aus that someone had to pay for fucking up? Was that aimed at him? And could he blame her for wanting to tell them the truth? He was the reason they had an army on their doorstep. They went straight for the exit he'd used. The exit they'd watched him use. Max rubbed his face. What should he do? A room filled with people already hostile to them being there. Fess up now and Aus would cut him down where he stood. But what if everyone else got punished because of his mistake?

"They were waiting for us," Artan said. "I don't know how, but they knew we'd pop up somewhere. I don't think they knew where the exit was, but—"

"They do now." Aus spoke through gritted teeth. "They're flushing us out like fucking rabbits." All of his crew were in the comms room with them. Most of them nodded their agreement. He leaned closer to the screen, focusing on the exit Artan and the others had come from. "They're making barriers like the others." He kicked the wall. "Fuck!"

"We need to keep our heads." Jan pointed at the screen,

his upper body even larger than usual. Swollen with extra layers. Probably body armour. And probably not enough of it to go around. Gracie and Aus didn't appear to be wearing any. "How many soldiers would you say we're dealing with here?"

"I reckon there's five hundred of them at the first hatch," Gracie said. "At a guess, I'd say there's another three hundred at the second hatch."

"We're screwed," Freddie said.

"And I know who to blame." Aus fixed on Gracie. "We didn't have these problems until you brought your friends here."

Max's pulse ran so fast his chest ached. His face grew hot. He stepped back towards the part of the room most in shadow. Maybe he should just tell them what he'd done. Get it over with. Gracie said someone would be punished. She'd rat him out eventually.

Gracie threw up a wild shrug. "Is it really the time for this, Aus?"

"If we're going to die, I want to have my fucking say."

"You *always* have your say. Also, don't forget, you were the one killing people in their homes when we stole the solar panels. Who's saying this isn't a retaliation for that? So why don't you try, just this once, not having your say? Unless you having your say contributes to the problem in front of us. See how that works out for you."

All because of him. Because he'd fucked up. Max stepped forwards. "Aus."

"What?"

"I—"

"You're ready to fight?" Gracie said. She stared at him. Into him. "That's good. We all need to be ready to act. Now we need to make a plan. Dad?"

Jan had continued to watch the screens. "With how

quickly they're putting up that barrier," he said, "I don't think we have a huge amount of time. Artan, Nick, Freddie, Jason, Rufus, Hawk, Olga, and Max, I want you to defend the tunnel against the new army. We need to move fast to get it ready. The rest of us will take the other side. We each need a pair of people doing supply runs between the tunnels and the armoury. We need to make sure we don't run out of ammo."

"And that's it?" Max said, his words erratic with his giddy pulse. "Less than ten people on each side?"

"Any more in each tunnel and there won't be room to fight," Jan said. "And if they find another way in, we'll need people ready to defend on those fronts. We'll take walkie-talkies. Gracie, I need you to co-ordinate from here." Jan handed Max a walkie-talkie. "Can you take this to the pleasure dome and give it to someone? We need to keep them informed too. I think we need to assume they have all our exits covered. At some point, we might have to use the escape hatch. Hopefully, because it comes out much farther than the other exits, they won't have it under surveillance. We'll have to let them know the best time to make a move."

"Is there ever a good time to come out amongst diseased?" Max said, the walkie-talkie heavy in his hand.

"No. But here's hoping the two armies make enough noise to call the diseased over to them. That they clear the way for us. Also, can you tell them we might need more soldiers? All the able-bodied need to be ready to fight."

Although he now had the walkie-talkie, Max still held his hand towards Jan as if offering it back to him.

"Can you do that for me, Max?"

Everyone watched him. He nodded and whispered a hoarse, "Yep."

"Right!" Jan brought his hands together with a *crack!* "Any questions?"

Silence.

"Okay, let's do this." Jan led Aus and his crew from the room.

William and Matilda, who were going with Jan and Aus, waited for the rest of them to leave before they quickly exchanged hugs with Artan, Hawk, Olga, and finally Max. William held onto Max and whispered, "You're going to be okay, man."

Butterflies tore through Max's stomach.

"Right." Artan took the lead, opened one of the armoury's doors, and handed over weapons. "We need to set up our tunnel like the other one. Partly closed doors. A shitload of ammo and guns at each point. The keys in the locks, ready to set off the explosives if the time comes."

Freddie leaned towards the monitors and said, "*When* the time comes."

Artan led them from the room. Max and Gracie remained.

"What the *fuck* was that about?" Gracie said.

"What?"

"I'm trying to keep you alive, and you're about to rat us both out to my prick of a brother."

"I was going to take the blame. I wanted to take the heat off you."

"Who was the one who covered up for you?"

Max's stomach sank. "I thought you were going to tell them what I'd done. You said someone would have to pay for leading the army here."

"Because that's what Aus needed to hear. Next time you're about to self-destruct, try to make it the very last resort, yeah? Get your fucking head straight. Now let the people in the pleasure dome know what's happening."

"I'm sorry, Gracie."

"Don't be sorry. Just don't fucking do it!"

CRACK! Whoosh! Adrenaline still tearing through him, Max entered the pleasure dome. The attention of the room spun his way. Between one and two hundred scared people. What news did he bring? His already knotted stomach twisted tighter. The reek of sick, sweat, and flatulence smothered him. The raw funk of fear.

Many of the people in the dome didn't have a fight in them. Too young or too old. Did they even have enough of them to defend an attack down a third tunnel? The escape hatch open in the centre of the room. A tight crawl through hell towards scores of diseased. They were screwed.

A man in his forties with a balding head and canted stance, which he propped up with a cane, stood near the open tunnel. He'd chosen a central position in the room. He must have fancied himself the leader. Max handed him the walkie-talkie. All the while, everyone stared at him. But at least they were just people. At least—

A small girl with blonde hair appeared on Max's right. Six or seven years old, she had blue eyes. Until they changed, vanishing beneath crimson lenses of blood. Her jaw twitched as if the need to bite stirred within her. He shook his head. "We need to wait."

The man holding the walkie-talkie said, "Wait for what? What are you talking about?"

"Sorry." Max turned his back on the little girl. "There's a chance we might need some more able-bodied people to help in this war. Can you get them ready so they're on standby?"

The man pointed at the escape hatch. "Why don't we crawl along this now?"

"We have to wait."

The man shrugged. "Like I said, wait for what?"

"The escape hatch leads us close to the wall."

"So?"

"The diseased."

"Huh?"

"That's where most of the diseased are. We need to make sure there's enough noise being made by the two armies before we take that path."

"Two?"

Should he have said that? "We're being attacked from two sides. We need to make sure they cause enough commotion to attract the diseased and drag them away from the wall before we risk leaving. We might not even need to leave immediately. Just be ready, okay?"

The small girl with the bleeding eyes had turned back into the small girl with the azure stare. She tugged on Max's shirt. "Are we going to die?"

Max lost his breath. For a second time, blood spread across her eyes. It ran down her pale cheeks like crimson molasses. He stumbled backwards, knocking into a lady.

"Ow!" The lady shoved him.

Max turned his back on the girl, dropped his head, and forced his way from the room. He hit the button to get out of there with a *crack* and called back, "Keep the walkie-talkie on. We'll be in contact."

Stumbling on tired legs, Max shook his head as he walked towards Artan's army. Whatever happened, he wouldn't be leaving via that escape hatch. Too tight. Too small. Too long. No chance.

Jason and Rufus ran from the armoury to the tunnel's open door. They both carried several guns each and took off towards Artan, Hawk, Freddie, and Nick at the other end near the hatch.

Once they'd passed, Olga followed, her backpack heavy with ammo. "Are you okay?"

"You're not fighting at the front?"

"No, I'm going to do the ammo runs with you. I want to make sure you're all right. So, are you okay?"

"Yes." The long tunnel stretched away from them. The two sets of double doors were partly closed. "Whatever happens, we need to beat these fuckers. We can't be sending the community down that escape hatch into a meadow filled with diseased."

Her skin pale, her eyes tight at the edges. "Are you sure you're ready for this?"

"No, I'm not." Max shook his head. Jason and Rufus took up their positions at the set of doors closest to them. "But I'm more ready for this than I am for the escape hatch. So we have to make this work. We have to win."

Every time Max had looked down any of Dout's corridors, either when he'd walked down them, or just from looking through the windows in the doors, they'd appeared impossibly long. An unnecessary distance. But now this tunnel didn't stretch anywhere near far enough.

They were about as ready as they could be. Olga and Max at the back by the last set of doors. Jason and Rueben by the next set. Hawk, Artan, Freddie, and Nick, the first line of defence. The silence so complete, the tunnel came close to being a vacuum.

Olga reached across to Max and laid her hand over the back of his. "We'll get through this."

Before he replied, someone hit the other side of the hatch at the end of the tunnel.

Bang!

CHAPTER 24

Bang! Artan flinched, the deep echo of the army's attack booming through the tunnel. A shower of dirt and grit fell, hitting him and the steel floor.

The stock of his makeshift gun pressed into his shoulder, and with Nick beside him, Artan closed one eye and looked up its barrel at the hatch. "That's a long way to fall. I can't see them getting down here, you know. I wouldn't mind betting they'll get that hatch open, get a face full of bullets, and give up when they realise the enormity of their task."

Bang!

Nick flinched from the raining grit. "And if they don't give up?"

Artan's finger tensed on the trigger. "Then we help persuade them."

"I dunno," Nick said. "I can't see them leaving."

"I know being below the enemy doesn't give us the best tactical advantage, but with the climb and how narrow the hatch is, I wouldn't trade places with them. And we have six more ways out of this place they're yet to find."

"Seven," Nick said. "We have the escape hatch too."

"See, we'll be fine."

Bang! Artan jumped again.

"Are you okay?" Nick said.

Artan's heart beat in his throat. "Not really, but we have to be, don't we? Everything will work out."

All the while, Nick had kept his gun pointed at the hatch.

Bang!

Artan stepped back and pulled Nick with him. Hawk and Freddie were directly behind them. They edged back too. About a third of a mile between them and the first set of partly closed doors.

Bang!

Stepping back again, Artan raised his eyebrows at Hawk and then Freddie. They both gripped their guns. They were both ready when needed. They'd work as a foursome, the two at the front firing until they ran out of bullets, and then they'd swap positions while the shooters reloaded.

Bang!

Clang!

The hatch landed with a splash of sparks. Artan gripped his gun. Nick remained beside him. He reached across and rested a hand on Nick's back. "Let's fucking do this."

A boot stepped onto the highest ladder rung. Artan opened fire. The gun shook and barked. The recoil sent him stumbling back into Hawk, who held him up.

The woman at the top of the ladder screamed, slipped, and fell.

Thud! She hit the ground hard, held her back, and writhed on the floor. Her wailing agony more diseased than human. Too many broken bones and ruptured organs. Another barking burst of gunfire, Nick shot her dead.

Everyone in the tunnel held their breath. Artan's pulse pounded in his ears. The top of the ladder remained clear.

Nick stepped closer, peering up through the hole.

Artan caught up to him.

His eyes wild, his face glistening with sweat, Nick pointed at where he looked.

Artan nodded.

Nick raised his right hand with three fingers held up. He used them to count down.

When he dropped his last finger, they charged forwards. Artan yelled, his gun bucking, shaking his entire body.

Cries and shouts above them. Another six soldiers fell, each of them hitting the ground like the woman before them.

Seconds later, Artan and Nick stepped back, and Artan called, "Reload." He pointed his gun at the ground and moved into the centre of the tunnel, so he and Nick rubbed shoulders while Hawk and Freddie flanked them. They took their position in front, pointed their guns up the ladders, and shot.

Adrenaline turned Artan clumsy. He dropped his ammo clip on the steel floor. He retrieved it and whacked it into place with a *clack!*

He drew deep breaths to counter the adrenaline rush. His ears rang even after Hawk and Freddie stopped shooting. A pile of fallen bodies on the ground in front of them. One or two still moved. Hawk and Freddie made sure they didn't.

Artan shouted, "This could work, you know! Are you ready for round two?"

Nick nodded.

Freddie and Hawk pulled into the centre of the tunnel. Shoulder to shoulder. They gave Artan space to pass Hawk on the left and Nick space to pass Freddie on the right.

It had been working so far, so Artan stepped forwards, pointed his weapon up, and halted. "Fuck!" He ran, hooked an arm around Nick, and dragged him away.

The flaming ball fell a second later, the dead bodies softening its landing. The size of a large pumpkin and made from tar, it belched thick black smoke, the toxic reek poisoning Artan's sinuses.

"What the fuck is that?" Freddie said.

The noxious ball set fire to the corpses' clothes. A splashing sound of liquid rained down behind it. The heady reek made Artan light-headed.

Whomp!

The flames grew and burned bright. The heat dragged sweat from Artan's pores. He stumbled back into Hawk. He pulled his shirt up to cover his nose and mouth. He could do nothing for his stinging eyes, tears mixing with the sweat on his face.

Hawk pulled Artan. Freddie did the same for Nick and said, "We need to get farther back. We can't do anything in this smoke."

∽

THE BODIES BURNED, the angry flames fuelled by the accelerant falling from the sky. Smoke thickened the air, but Artan and the others had pulled back far enough to be away from the worst of it. They were close to the first set of doors. They could blow this tunnel whenever they wanted.

Clang!

"What's that?" Hawk said.

His eyes still streaming, Artan blinked repeatedly, but the thick smoke had reduced his visibility to almost zero.

Clang!

Hawk squeezed past Artan, shouldered his gun, and sent several shots down the corridor. They hit metal.

"Shields," Freddie said. "They've got fucking shields."

The scrape of metal against metal. Of shields sliding along the steel floor as they pressed forwards, still enshrouded in smoke.

"And they sound heavy," Nick said. "Resilient."

"So we have no chance of penetrating them?" Artan said.

"I don't think so. But they'll also have a hard time moving them."

The edge of the cloud of black smoke stirred before revealing the first shield. Thin and wide, it ran from wall to wall and would have easily passed through the hatch.

"It looks like one of the panels they've used to make their fences up top," Hawk said. He fired on them again. It halted their progress.

"Keep shooting." Freddie clenched his jaw and sent a spray of bullets into the shield. "It's keeping them pinned back."

Hawk and Freddie pulled into the middle to reload while a shield appeared above the first one. Men and women shouted in a language Artan didn't understand. He shot through the space between the two, and the top barrier fell forwards with a *clang!*

Artan and Nick opened fire on the soldiers jumping over the first barrier. Several more went down before they raised the fallen shield. The barrels of several guns appeared over the top. "Shit!" Artan said. "Pull back! Pull back!"

Nick ran through the doors last, chased by the enemy's bullets. Hawk and Freddie lay on their stomachs and returned fire. Artan stepped behind one of the partly closed doors, his walkie-talkie in hand, his throat tight from smoke inhalation. He coughed several times. "Gracie, it's Artan. Can you hear me?"

"Yes. How's it going?"

Clang! Another barrier hit the steel floor. The army moved closer. A few feet at a time. Slow and inevitable. They'd reach the doors soon.

"Not great," Artan said. "We're going to have to shut this section off and blow it up."

"When will you have to make that choice?"

"We have a small amount of time."

"Fine, give me a minute, yeah?"

Minutes lasted hours down here. Artan waited. The stuttered clack of Hawk's and Freddie's guns. The ring of their enemy's bullets hitting the partly closed steel doors.

∼

"Artan?"

He raised the walkie-talkie. "Yep, go on, Gracie."

"I've spoken to Dad, and he said they're having similar issues."

"So what do we do?"

"Hold on as long as you can. Get as many of them down there with you. And then blow the place to smithereens."

CHAPTER 25

William shook his left hand and then his right. They both buzzed with the vibrations of firing his gun. His knuckles ached, and his eyes burned from the thick smoke. He stood in front of the wheel to close the doors, Matilda beside him with the walkie-talkie.

"It sounds like they've pre-planned this," Gracie said. "Artan said they're doing the same on his side. Fireballs. Shields…"

"Close the doors so there's only a crack left," Jan said. The man projectile-sweated and gnashed his teeth. Aus at his side, they stood closest to the enemy by the partly closed doors. As they should; after all, Jan had body armour on. Not that he'd admitted it.

William turned the handle, closing the gap to just a few inches. Just wide enough for Jan's gun.

Jan poked the end through and pulled the trigger. The gun shook, clattering against the doors on either side. He shouted over the clacking chaos, "William, Aus, get on the keys. We need to be ready to blow this place."

The *ting* of bullet fire against their enemy's shields. It

drew closer with the army's progress.

William held the key on his side of the corridor in a pinch. He watched their attackers through the window in the door. They'd streamlined their advance. Improved their technique. Where some had fallen, they now slid the steel barrier over without exposing themselves. The screech of metal slid over metal. The slam of the heavy shields landed on the other side.

Jan threw down his gun and took Matilda's while she reloaded the one he'd discarded.

When Matilda had finished, Jan shouted, "Speak to Gracie. We need to know when to blow this place. We want as many of them in the tunnel as possible before we bring the ceiling down."

Screech! Clang! The army continued its slow and inevitable progress. Closing in on them. Ready to crush them.

Matilda, red-faced, her knuckles white on the black walkie-talkie. "Gracie!" She shrugged at William before trying again. "Gracie!"

"What's happening?" Jan said.

"She's not responding."

"Here!" Jan stepped aside and handed Matilda his gun. She posted it through the slot and fired.

Jan gripped the walkie-talkie and screamed, "Gracie! Come in, Gracie. What's going on?"

Screech! Clang! Screech! Clang!

Matilda's gun ran out. William moved away from the key and picked up the one she'd loaded for Jan, swapping them around before he reloaded the gun she'd given him. How long could they keep this up? They'd have to blow the tunnel soon.

Jan bellowed into the walkie-talkie as if repetition would yield different results. "Gracie! Gracie! Gracie!"

CHAPTER 26

"Gracie's not answering," Max said.

"How do you know?" Olga weaved from left to right as if it would help her see better along the tunnel.

"Look at the way Artan's holding his walkie-talkie. He's clearly not getting a response. I know we need to keep the channels clear, but will you try to get a hold of her?"

Olga sighed and raised the walkie-talkie to her mouth. It released a static hiss when she pressed the button. "Gracie?"

"Who's that?" Jan's authoritative bark came through to them.

"O-Olga."

"We told you to keep the line clear. We're struggling to contact Gracie as it is."

Max took the walkie-talkie. "That's why we're checking. We wanted to be certain there was a problem before we did anything. Olga and I will go to the surveillance room now to see what's happening. If nothing else, we can give her a working walkie-talkie. Over."

Keeping hold of the walkie-talkie, Max led the way

around the corridor surrounding the pleasure dome. *Clack!* He hit the button to open the door to the surveillance room. *Whoosh!* The door slid aside.

"Gracie!" She stood alone in front of the screens. Her arms hung limp by her sides. The two monitors watching each hatch were filled with people. The camera didn't have a wide enough lens to fit them all in. Both screens showed a steady stream of each army lining up and climbing into Dout. A steady stream of invaders descending into the tunnels.

Max nudged her. "Gracie."

She spun on him, her teeth bared, her lip raised in a snarl. Her skin had turned so pale, she'd gone damn near translucent.

"What's going on?" Max said.

Her eyes glazed and her jaw loose, Gracie shook her head. "We're screwed." Her voice broke, and tears stood in her eyes when she pointed at the screens. "How on earth are we supposed to defend against that? Even if we blow up the corridors, there's too many of them. It won't stop them."

Despite his hammering heart and shallow breaths, Max forced calm. He needed to keep his head. *Mad Max*. No, he had this. "It might not stop them, Gracie. But it will slow them down, and that's the best we have in this moment."

"Gracie!" Jan's voice came from the walkie-talkie on the desk.

Artan joined the chorus. "Gracie, we need some guidance down here."

"I've lived here my entire life," Gracie said. "This is where Mum died."

"Gracie." Max held her hands. Her gnarled and twitching hands. No, they were her hands. Soft. Gentle. *Mad Max*. "Gracie," he started again, the pressure of Olga's touch on his back, "now isn't the time to be mourning the loss of this place. We need to survive first. There will be plenty of time to think about what's been lost"—*Mad Max*—"trust me."

The glaze fogging Gracie's green eyes cleared, revealing the woman he knew.

"There we go," Max said. He picked up the walkie-talkie from her desk and handed it to her. "You're in here because you're the best person for the job. Now, tell them what they need to hear so they can make a decision."

"Uh—"

"Gracie, love, is that you?" Jan said.

"Y-yes."

"Are you okay?"

Her brow wrinkled and her voice wavered before she found her strength and asserted, "There are a lot of soldiers above ground still. We need to blow the tunnels, but we need to do it when they're as full as they can be. Right now, they're still climbing down the ladders like there's plenty of room. I'll watch them and let you know when they stop sending people down."

"Okay, sweetheart. I'm glad you're back."

Gracie let go of the button of the side of the walkie-talkie. Her arms fell limp at her sides again.

"We might be okay," Olga said.

"Look at the screens," Gracie said.

And she had a point. Max's stomach turned somersaults as the armies on both sides flooded into Dout. One after the other, they climbed down the ladders. They wouldn't be in this mess were it not for him. The walkie-talkie he'd taken from Olga in his hand, he pointed the aerial at her. "Olga, you stay here and help Gracie decide when they need to blow the tunnels." He returned to the door and hit the button to open it.

"Where are you going?" Olga said.

Max stepped out into the corridor. "I have a plan. I'll stay in touch."

CHAPTER 27

They'd wound the doors closed so just a small gap remained. A gap wide enough for Artan to slip the barrel of his gun through and shoot. When he ran out of ammo, he stepped aside, and Nick took his place. Hawk waited to go next while Artan reloaded. Most of their bullets hit the army's steel shields, but it forced caution from them and slowed their advance. They couldn't hope for much more.

The window in the door on Artan's side had several black marks on it from where it had stood up to the army's attack. So far, the doors had held like Jan had promised. How would they fare when they blew up the corridor? The enemy a matter of feet away, they were about to find out. He pressed the button on the side of the walkie-talkie. "How's it looking up there, Gracie?"

Even the static hiss made him jump. "They're still coming in."

"I'm not sure how much longer we can wait." Artan held the key in a pinch. Freddie did the same on the other side of the tunnel. He watched Artan with unblinking eyes, ready to bring down tonnes of steel and earth on the enemy.

"Nick," Artan said, "it's time to close the doors."

Nick's eyes roved as if he couldn't focus on anything. But he gripped the wheel and turned it. "Ask Gracie how long we have left."

"We need to trust her, Nick. She's telling us to hold off."

"What's Jan doing?"

"Tilly," Artan said to his walkie-talkie, "when are you going to turn the keys?"

CHAPTER 28

The faces of their enemy pressed up against the windows. Pure hatred. They made the diseased look passive. Just inches from William. They hit the other side of the doors with the buts of their guns. Steel clanged against steel.

"Gracie," Matilda said into her walkie-talkie. Jan watched her, his eyes wide. "We need to make a choice soon. Are they slowing down yet?"

"Okay, okay. I think they're ..." Gracie went quiet.

William held one key, and Aus held the other.

The slight hiss of static, Gracie said, "Now!"

They turned the keys.

Whomp!

It started at the far end of the tunnel, near the ladders. The soldiers screamed.

Whomp!
Whomp!
Whomp!

Fiery explosions raced towards them, galloping along the

tunnel. The soldiers writhed and fought one another as if they could avoid being cremated where they stood.

Whomp!

The brightest glow of the lot dazzled William and left flashing lights in his vision. Rubbing his sore eyes, he swallowed against the smokey taste seared into the back of his throat from the enemy's flaming bombs. Heat radiated from the locked doors.

As William's sight cleared, Jan said it before he could. "The tunnel's still standing. Shit!"

The ceiling and walls hadn't collapsed like they'd planned. The soldiers were down, their bodies on fire, but … "How long before they realise we've just played our ace?" William said.

"Gracie?" Matilda's voice trembled. "We've blown the tunnel, but it hasn't collapsed."

Artan spoke next. "Same here. It's baked every soldier in the place, but it won't stop the others coming down."

"Shit!" Gracie said. "Well, they've stopped rushing into the tunnel for now."

Jan growled, "But it's only a matter of time." He stamped on the steel floor. "Fuck!" He took the walkie-talkie from Matilda, pressed the button, and used his free hand to shoo the rest of them away from the hot doors. "Gracie, sweetheart." From rage to the soft tones of a caring father. How William would have loved to have his dad beside him right now. "I need you to tell us when they come down again, okay?"

"W-what will you do?"

"Fight them."

"But we can't win. We need to retreat."

"We'll make that decision when we have to. It's not an easy call to send all those kids and vulnerable people into the wilderness. We need to make sure there are no diseased waiting for them."

"I might be able to help with that."

Jan stared at the walkie-talkie.

"Max?" William said. He took the small black device from Jan. "What's going on?"

Max's voice echoed. "I'm in the escape tunnel."

"You're *what?!*"

"I'll let you know what it's like out here in case we need to evacuate. But I'm hoping it won't come to that."

"What are you going to do?"

"I'm going to send the diseased over the armies' barriers."

"Shit!" William sagged where he stood. "Are you sure that's a good idea?"

"You have a better one?"

Matilda shrugged at William, who sighed and shook his head. "No, we don't. Good luck, man."

CHAPTER 29

Of course Max didn't want to crawl for two fucking miles on his stomach, but they were under attack because of him. He had about a foot clearance on either side and above. The faint glow from the open hatch behind, his elbows sore from the unforgiving steel surrounding him. His panting gasps echoed in the tight space.

Mad Max.

Pains streaked along the base of his skull from where he crawled with his head raised. His eyes burned from staring into the darkness. Red eyes stared back at him. Clawing hands pawed at him.

Mad Max.

"It's not real." He shook his head. "It's not fucking real."

Something hissed in his ear.

He lost his breaths for a second. "It's not real!"

Clack! Snapping teeth to his right. He moved left.

Clang! His skull rang from where he smashed it against the left wall.

The walkie-talkie hissed. "Max?" Olga's voice. "How are you doing?"

"I—" He lost his words and coughed to clear his throat. "I'm okay."

"How much farther do you have to go?"

"I don't know. It's dark down here." Talking robbed the air from his lungs, but at least he had the comfort of her voice.

Olga said, "I'll check back in soon."

The static hiss of connection cut off, and Max whimpered. "Stay."

But he'd be okay. He could do this. He'd done it many times before. The Asylum. Edin. His mum. His dad. His brothers. A sharp shake of his head as if he could flick the thoughts aside. He pressed the button on his walkie-talkie. "Have they sent in the next wave yet?"

"Not yet," Gracie said.

For the second time in as many minutes, Max slammed head-first into steel. His skull rang like a struck bell. Damp with his own sweat, his eyes burned. He reached up and pressed his palm against the inside of the closed hatch. He raised it an inch. The glow from the moon shone like a spotlight compared to the dark void of the tunnel.

His last chance to change his mind. If only he could. He let the hatch resettle and pressed the button on his walkie-talkie. "Artan?"

"Hi, Max. How are you doing?"

"Fine. I'm going to go to William's side first, okay? They have a larger army to fight off over there."

"Okay, I understand."

"And, Gracie?"

"Yep?"

"I'm going to turn off my walkie-talkie. You'll have to direct them from what you're seeing on the screens."

"Are you okay?"

"I'm fine. Just keep an eye on what's going on."

"All right. Good luck, Max."

Max turned the dial on the side of his walkie-talkie, cutting it off with a gentle *click!* Whatever happened, he had to try. He'd nearly lost himself once. Maybe he would lose himself for sure this time. But this was bigger than him. One last breath to fill his lungs, he opened the hatch and crawled out into the night.

CHAPTER 30

Artan and the others joined Jason and Rufus at the second set of doors. They brought back all the spare guns and ammo they'd used for the first wave and placed them with what already lay there. With Olga's help, Jason and Rufus had made sure they were well stocked for the second phase.

Hawk, as the last of them, set down the guns he'd carried before Artan led them back to the closed steel doors. This time, Jason and Rufus joined them.

"Forgive me," Rufus said to Freddie, "but what's going on?"

"We blew the tunnel," Freddie said with a sigh. "It didn't collapse."

"So they're going to come back down here?" Jason said.

Freddie nodded. "I'd say that's a safe assumption."

"And what will we do then?"

"We pull back to the second set of doors," Artan said, "and we fight them from there."

"But what I don't get," Freddie said, "is why *Max* is going outside the community."

Nick's attention burned brighter than anyone's. Artan had kept the secret for so long, that now, even with Max's permission, he still had to force the words out. "Max has powers."

"We're not kids, you know?" Freddie's frown threw lines along his brow, and his mohawk shifted forwards.

"What do you mean?"

"Powers? *Seriously,* Artan? What is he, a fucking superhero?"

"In a way."

"What?"

"He's immune," Hawk said.

Everyone, save for Artan and Hawk, stopped dead. After a few steps, Artan also halted and turned around.

Nick's line of questioning came with less aggression than Freddie's, the hard walls attaching the tail of an echo to his low tones. "What are you talking about?" The sides of his eyes pinched.

"Look," Artan said.

Freddie stormed up to him with heavy steps. "Why didn't you say something sooner?"

Artan stepped so close to Freddie, their noses damn near touched. The shorter man might have been built like a boulder, and he probably weighed twice as much as Artan, but Artan held his ground. He delivered a slow and measured reply. "I didn't say anything because Max didn't want me to."

"Sounds a bit fucking selfish if you ask me."

Nick pulled Freddie back.

"Max got bitten back home in Edin. When he didn't turn, they made him a lab rat. They locked him up and ran tests on him. Since then, he's been quite guarded with his secret. When people find out, they get a strange sense of entitlement over him. As if his immunity is a public asset."

"You don't think it is?" Freddie said.

"Were you in his shoes, would you want to be locked up and tested on? Would you want to be treated as both the hope for humanity and an animal that needs to be locked away in case you're carrying the infection?"

"I didn't think about that." Freddie quietened for a moment before the fire returned to his dark glare. "And you thought it was acceptable to bring him into this community when he could have turned us all?"

"You're proving my point," Artan said. "We *know* he's not dangerous. We don't need to seek counsel on that. And as for what use he is to this community … have you seen the state he's in?"

"Of course. He's a wreck."

"That's from helping us like he's about to help everyone in Dout. That's the cost of his immunity. In this world, you get into tight spots. As much as we didn't want to rely on Max, when we needed him, he stepped up. Every time."

"Boo-hoo!" Freddie said.

Hawk charged at Freddie.

Artan wrapped an arm around him and dragged him back. While holding onto him, he said, "I get why you're pissed. Freddie's being a prick—"

"I heard that!"

"You were supposed to." And then back to Hawk. "Just give me a moment to explain, okay?"

Hawk chewed the inside of his mouth.

"Okay?" Artan said.

Hawk finally nodded, raised his hands, and stepped away.

"Now, Freddie," Artan said, "you need to understand—"

"Don't tell me—"

"Shut *up*, Freddie," Nick said. "Some of us want to hear what Artan's saying."

Freddie's lips tightened, and he folded his arms across his chest.

"Max has already saved our lives more times than I can remember," Artan said. "He's gone into crowds of diseased and killed one after the other. *Hundreds* of diseased."

Freddie shrugged. "We've all killed diseased."

"Do you ever fucking shut up?" Hawk said.

"But we haven't all stood shoulder to shoulder with them," Artan said. "We haven't been turned slick by the slime and puss from their infected cuts. We haven't had them snarl and hiss in our ears, felt their foetid breath on our cheeks. We haven't all killed our mums and dads or our brothers to put them out of their misery." Artan flinched at the image of his dead dad. The blood in their front room.

Dropping his crossed arms, Freddie said, "Does Aus know?"

"He has Tilly and William with him, so he will do now."

"And you think, in his current state of mind, Max will be any help to us?"

"Like has already happened so many times with Max, he's our only hope. He either helps or he doesn't. It doesn't change what we have to do down here."

"And he hasn't let us down yet," Hawk said. "But he also hasn't been this damaged before. The kid's been through a lot."

"For now," Artan said, turning his back on the others and continuing towards the locked doors up ahead, "we have to put our faith in him." He reached the window, the glass dark with smoke damage. Charred lumps on the floor that had once been the enemy.

Nick arrived next to Artan, the others catching up a second later.

"Max knows what he needs to do," Artan said, "and he'll give everything he's got to help us."

CHAPTER 31

Enough time had passed for the doors to cool down. William cupped his face to shut out the light and peered through the window in the left door. Several shields, pockmarked with bullet holes, lay amongst the charred corpses of hundreds of soldiers. "It's hard not to look at all those burned bodies."

"Don't worry," Aus said when he peered through the window in the other door, "I'm sure there will be more live ones down here soon."

"Max will do what's needed."

"I wish I had your confidence."

"Why not be hopeful?" William said.

"Because it might stop you preparing for war."

"Don't worry about that. I know we have a fight ahead of us. Jeez!" William jumped back from the window. Even from a third of a mile away, the vibration from the body hitting the ground ran through the soles of his boots.

"What was that?" Jan peered over William's shoulder.

Thud! Thud! Thud! Soldiers hit the ground around the base of the ladder. Others climbed down, the first of which reached the bottom and ran towards them. A short woman with a tight ponytail, she watched her steps, picking her path through her burned comrades and the fallen shields.

A steady stream of soldiers followed her, jumping from the ladder like she had. The front runners were now only fifty feet from the locked doors, but they had their backs turned on William and the others and watched where they'd come from. Bodies rained from the sky.

One soldier, a tall man with a bald head, jumped from the ladder, took one step along the tunnel, and a body landed on top of him. His neck bent too far one way, and he turned instantly flaccid. William rubbed the back of his own neck as both soldiers became more bodies in an ever-growing mound.

"I'm guessing Max got to them, then?" Aus said.

Matilda currently held the walkie-talkie. "Max? Max, what's going on? Are you there, Max?"

More and more soldiers backed towards the locked doors. About one hundred, maybe more. The closest now about forty feet away. Fewer climbed down the ladders, but the bodies continued to fall.

∽

THE MOUND of corpses stood about ten feet tall. Each person landed differently on the uneven pile. Many of them bent in ways no body should. The doors might have muted the cracks from breaking spines and necks, but William still flinched with every landing.

"Look!" Aus said.

One body on the top of the pile twitched. Its arm snapped out with a spasm. Another one twitched next to it.

More people rained down while the two twitchers crawled free of the corpse mound.

The pile grew. One in every two fallen bodies landed and reanimated. Some of them rolled free from the small hill. Some of them stood on wobbly legs and stumbled away.

They held their familiar canted posture. One shoulder higher than the other, they slashed at the air and charged.

The soldiers fought them with guns, mowing down the creatures. But for every diseased that fell, two more rained from above.

"It's worked!" William slapped Aus on the back. "I told you he'd do it."

Matilda pressed the walkie-talkie. "We've not heard from Max, but he's sent the diseased down our side. These soldiers don't have long left. Hold tight, Artan, I'm sure he's com—"

"Oh, shit!" Jan said.

While the soldiers held the diseased back, those behind them grabbed two of the shields the first wave had brought down with them.

"The soldiers are fighting back." Matilda still had the walkie-talkie in her hand. "They're using their shields to set up a barrier against the diseased."

Gracie came in with a sharp hiss of static. "Do you think they'll succeed?"

William shrugged at Matilda. How could he tell?

"I think they will," Jan said.

The soldiers moved closer to William and the others. The shields held the diseased back for now. But even if they did keep the creatures at bay, they were still trapped.

Adrenaline sent William's pulse through the roof. Several soldiers carried another shield towards them as if they expected to defend against Dout and the diseased. One soldier, a woman with bulging biceps, held a device that had a handle and cogs on one end, and a long flat steel paddle on the other. "What are they doing?"

They slid the shield into place before the woman shoved

the steel paddle over the top, forcing it through the tiny gap where the two doors met.

The paddle, about an inch thick and a foot wide, slipped through the slit. Aus kicked it several times, bending the end.

The woman wound the handle, her already swollen biceps engorged with her effort. The cogs clacked and the flat paddle split along its thin side, prizing the doors apart.

Aus kicked them again, but the two sides of the paddle stretched wider, forcing the doors with it.

Jan stepped back. "Even if we try to shoot them through that gap, their shields will protect them. We have to retreat."

William dragged Matilda with them while she spoke into her walkie-talkie. "We're pulling back. They're using some kind of tool to force the doors open."

William, Matilda, Jan, and Aus reached the partly closed second set of doors. They had ammo and weapons, but nothing that could penetrate a shield. And now the army had a way of opening the doors, it would just be a matter of time before they were overrun.

"So much for that fucking plan," Jan said. He stamped on the floor. "Fuck it!" He snatched the walkie-talkie from Matilda. "Gracie?"

"Yep."

"Did Max tell you if the escape hatch is clear?"

"He's been dark since you last heard him."

"Can you see anything on the cameras that might help us work out if it's safe?"

Gracie sighed. "You know I can't see the end of the escape hatch. And in every other camera, I can see diseased. Lots of diseased. Maybe they've been dragged away from the escape hatch, but I don't know."

"Shit!" Jan said. "Freddie, can you hear me?"

"Yes, Jan."

"You need to get ready for the next wave. If your lot are

anything like ours, they have a tool to get them through the locked doors. Take them down before they can do that. Gracie?"

"Yes, Dad?"

"Do what you can to get a hold of Max. The plan hasn't worked. We need to contact him so he doesn't send the diseased down on Freddie's side. It'll only make things worse."

The clack of the turning cogs continued up ahead. The gap in the doors nearly wide enough to let the soldiers and their shield through. William grabbed Matilda's hand. They'd gotten away with a lot over these past few months. Maybe their luck had finally run out.

CHAPTER 32

If Max turned on his walkie-talkie now, the enemy would surely hear him. And what did he need to tell them? He'd done what he'd promised so far, so there was no need to talk to anyone inside Dout. He'd sent the diseased over the barriers on one side. Now he needed to do the other side and he was done. The plan was simple: get to their barrier, send the diseased over, and find somewhere to wash off the vile stench. Simple. Yeah, right.

Max's trousers were damp from the dew coating the long grass, the thick fabric chafing his cold skin. But no matter how many times he'd rubbed his hands against the sodden material, he couldn't remove the diseased's foetid imprint. Their stink. Their ooze. It had gone much deeper than surface level.

"Keep going." He said it to himself as he ran, the grass whipping at his legs, the moon his only guidance. "Keep going."

Max slowed to a halt on the brow of a small hill. The meadow stretched away from him. Several clusters of trees dotted the landscape like large clumps of broccoli. Impenetrable darkness around their bases, their tops dusted by the moon's silver glow. A fence similar to the one used by the first army sat as another clump in the meadow. The diseased gathered around the barrier. A smaller army than the first by about half, but an army nonetheless. Keep his head and everything would be fine.

Max drew close enough to hear the waiting soldiers over the frenzied snarls and growls of the diseased. They shouted to one another in a language he didn't recognise. A language completely different to that spoken by the first army. Some of them cried, the faint reek of their charred comrades still perfuming the air. The ravenous diseased pressed against their barrier.

The long grass swished. Heavy footfalls to Max's right. He spun just as diseased stumbled past him. Clumsy, phlegmy, it ran at the edge of its balance. As always, it had no interest in him.

Mad Max! He slammed his knuckles against the side of his head. "Get out. You won't do this to me now." His bottom lip buckled. "Please get out. I'm nearly done." He wiped his left hand against his left trouser leg again, swapped his walkie-talkie over and did the same with his right. Maybe he should check in? What if they needed to tell him something?

"What are you thinking?" Easier to whisper it aloud than to string a thought together in his chaotic mind. *Mad Max.* "Just execute the fucking plan. You're the reason this has happened. Stop being a fuck-up and fix it." The last thing he needs to be doing is alerting the army to his presence by turning on his walkie-talkie.

Max closed in on the barrier surrounding the army. The uneven ground sloped downhill towards their camp. He lifted one shoulder higher than the other and slashed at the air. Just another diseased in a sea of the fuckers.

Slamming into the twisting bodies at the back of the

stinking crowd, Max shoved his way through. They gathered around the army like the others had. Six or seven deep, they pressed against the barriers, but their collective weight did little to compromise the fence's integrity.

While closing his eyes, Max turned sideways between two diseased. One of them snarled at him and bit an irritable snap of their teeth. *Clack!*

But Max pushed on. Twisting and turning, forcing his way through. He made the gaps he needed, all while inhaling the rich vinegar tang of the monsters.

Max?

"Drake?" The closest brother to him in age. "Oh, Drake, I'm—no! It's not you. I know it's not you."

Max?

Max leaned closer to the next diseased that spoke to him. Cyrus stared back, but he held the creature's glare, and the image of his old friend faded. Replaced by the all too familiar crimson glaze of hatred. A woman, she had long and greasy hair. The gash in the side of her face revealed her jawbone. They couldn't keep on doing this. He wouldn't be a victim of their torment.

Max? His dad this time.

Just one row of diseased between him and the fence, Max bent down, linked his hands together beneath the beast masquerading as his father, and he boosted the creature over the top. The one next to it took the form of his mum. He sent her over too. They both hit the ground. The soldiers screamed.

While the diseased snarled and the soldiers fought them, Max sent more of the creatures over. Every one of them another person he'd known. But they weren't them. And he shouldn't feel guilty that he'd survived. He'd trade places in a heartbeat.

Diseased after diseased, the snarling and growling on the

inside of the fence turned into screaming chaos. Max operated with machine-like efficiency, sending over one and then the next.

And it didn't matter who stared back at him. They were all diseased fucks. They were a weapon. They didn't get to dictate his actions to him anymore.

"Fuck you!" He sent the next one over.

"Fuck you!" And then the next.

"Fuck you!"

Tears soaked his cheeks. But the diseased had lost their power over him. They weren't the people he once loved. He'd stared the monsters down and he'd won. When they got through this, and when William asked him and Olga if they wanted to go with them to the wall. This time he'd say yes. This time, he'd be ready.

CHAPTER 33

"Max!" Artan's knuckles ached from where he clung onto his walkie-talkie. "Max, can you hear me? What's going on up there?" Nick, Freddie, and Hawk stood around him. He peered through the window, cloudy with smoke damage, but not so cloudy it hid the burned bodies littering the floor. He had to squint to see the ladder rungs at the end of the tunnel. They'd sent Jason and Rufus over to William and Matilda to help with the fighting there. If they needed them, they'd call them back. Hopefully, they wouldn't need them.

"Artan?" Matilda's crackly voice came through to him. "How's it going?"

"We can't get a hold of Max."

"Then you need to pull back."

"We must be able to do something. What happened in your corridor? I struggled to follow over the walkie-talkies."

"The soldiers came down, clearly running away from the diseased. Some of them climbed, and some of them fell."

"*Fell?*" Artan said.

"Yeah, they didn't do so well. The ones who made it down

here picked up the shields they'd used against us and turned them on the diseased that followed them."

"Why didn't you shoot the soldiers?" Hawk said.

"Because we thought the diseased would finish them off. We didn't expect the soldiers to hold them back, and we didn't expect them to pry the doors open."

Artan drew a breath to reply, but stopped when Hawk put his hand over the walkie-talkie. "It sounds like their shields are the key."

"Tilly," Artan said, "we'll come back to you," and then to Hawk, "So what's your point?"

"Isn't it obvious? If we engage them in a gunfight, they'll shoot back, and they might get to the shields before we can take them down."

"So what's your point?" Artan said.

"Open the doors. Let me take their shields. If they don't have them, the diseased will do the hard work for us."

Freddie shook his head. "Are you mad?"

"You realise the diseased and soldiers are coming this way, right? We have no contact with Max, so he will send them down here like he did the others."

"That's what I'm worried about," Freddie said. "What if you get caught down there with them?"

"The longer we take to decide, the more likely that is to happen."

The walkie-talkie hissed when Artan pressed it.

Hawk took the radio from him. "What more can they tell you? We're wasting time. Also, I'm not asking for your permission, I'm simply telling you to let me through. This will work, trust me. I know Aus didn't select me—"

"*That's* what this is about?"

"But I have some good ideas," Hawk said.

"I didn't say you didn't."

Hawk shook with the force of his words. "Just open the fucking doors, Artan! We're running out of time."

Nick stepped between them. "What if we have to make a decision? What if you get in a situation we can't help you get out of?"

"Then lock me in with them. I know the consequences. Now let me through."

Artan shook his head while he opened the doors. "This is on you. We will lock you in there if we need to. *I* will."

"Good." Hawk bounced on the spot. "Now stop talking and hurry the fuck up."

Artan grunted with the effort of turning the wheel. When the gap between the doors had grown large enough for Hawk, he turned sideways and forced his way through, sprinting down the corridor to the first shield.

With the doors open, Artan had a much clearer view of the ladder at the end of the tunnel. His throat dried. His heart hammered. Could they really lock these doors if Hawk ran out of time? He pressed the button on his walkie-talkie. "Hawk's gone into the corridor to remove their shields before they get down here."

"He's *what?*" Matilda said.

"It's the right call. If it works," Artan said, "it will neutralise their threat to us. We'll be able to come over to your side to help you out."

CHAPTER 34

"He's done *what?*" William said. They were behind the second set of doors. Aus and Jan were still on the other side, like they were considering fighting the army.

"Hawk's gone to get the shields," Matilda said.

"They've opened the doors and let him through?"

"Yep."

Moe, one of Aus' team, nodded. "It makes sense." He shrugged. "If they can get the shields out of there before the soldiers come down on them."

"But if Hawk fails …" Matilda shook her head. "I know Artan. He won't close the doors."

"Even if he doesn't," Moe said, "Freddie will."

"We have to help them," Matilda said.

"What?" Moe said.

William showed Moe the palm of his hand. They weren't asking for his input. "There's nothing we can do for them now." The slow *clack* of turning cogs up ahead. They'd opened the gap in the doors to about six inches wide. "We have our own shit to deal with."

Jan ran at the opening doors. He shoved his gun through the gap and fired.

But the army had the protection of their shield. They returned fire. Aus and Jan pressed themselves against the walls. William pulled Matilda aside as bullets shot past them and hit the closed doors at the end of the tunnel.

When Jan stepped towards the opening doors again, Aus pulled him back. "Come on, Dad." He led the retreat, his dad behind him.

Aus reached William and the others, but Jan had halted about halfway along the tunnel. Aus threw his arms up. "What are you doing?"

Jan's brow wrinkled. His already warm gaze softened. The *clack* of the doors being forced open echoed in the tight tunnel. He shook his head. "We have to stop them getting through." He turned back towards the first set of doors and opened fire.

The bark of rapid fire responded. Jan twitched, stumbled back, and fell.

"*Dad!*" Aus stepped towards his father.

The first soldier squeezed through the gap and shot him again in the chest. Just to make sure. He then spun the wheel to open the doors.

"*Dad!*"

Two more of Aus' crew, Warren and Sam, grabbed Aus and pulled him back. As much as William would have done it if required, best it came from his friends. Sam spoke with soft tones. "He's gone, mate."

"No!" Aus shook his head and twisted to get free from his friends' restraint.

William flinched when a spray of bullets hit the doors directly next to his face. Another soldier had followed the first through the gap and fired on them.

Warren and Sam pulled Aus to the side. Moe helped restrain him.

"Aus!" Sam shouted this time, grunting as he fought to hold him back. "Listen. He's gone."

A wild beast, Aus snarled and twisted, writhed and bucked. "Let me go! I need to get his body."

"It's suicide," Sam said.

"I don't care."

"William," Sam said, "get Gracie on the walkie-talkie."

He held the radio to his mouth and pressed the button. "Gracie! Gracie! It's William."

"What's happening?" Gracie said.

William handed the walkie-talkie to Aus.

It settled the large man, instantly robbing him of his rage. "He's dead, Gracie!"

Moe turned the wheel to close their doors. More bullets sprayed against them.

"Who's dead?"

"Dad!"

The stamp of the enemy closed in. The clack of the turning wheel as Moe shut them out.

"What do you mean?"

"Dead, Gracie!" Aus shook, his voice echoing in the tunnel. "He's fucking dead. What part of that don't you understand? I need to get the body."

Sam took the walkie-talkie. "To get his body will put us all at risk, Gracie."

William pressed his face to the window. The enemy swarmed through the open doors. Those at the front had their guns raised, but they held their fire. The attack would be nothing more than wasted ammo against the now closed doors.

"Talk some sense into him, won't ya?" Sam said. "It's not what your dad would have wanted."

Aus balled his fists. "How the fuck do you—"

"Aus," Gracie said, cutting him off before he could get going, "Sam's right. Dad would want you to make the best decision for the sake of the community."

Jan lay on his back in the corridor. About halfway between them and the enemy. A kind and gentle leader. William hadn't known him long, but the scene before him took the air from his lungs and tightened his throat.

Clack! Aus dropped the radio. He fell against the wall before sliding down it into a sitting position.

While Aus remained on the floor, William helped load up the others with their ammo and weapons. Time to retreat again.

Aus returned to the closed doors. He rested his forehead against the glass. "It's such a fucking waste. What was he doing? We both could have gotten to safety." He punched the door. "Why did he throw his fucking life away?"

The attacking army carried the tool they'd used to open the doors. Three of them worked on fixing it while more soldiers swarmed around them. Two held it while one stood on the bend to straighten it out. About one hundred soldiers were now in the second section, every one of them armed. Even with the weapons and ammo Artan and the others had stolen, they were outnumbered and outgunned.

"With or without Dad," Aus said, "we're fucked. They'll get through the next few sets of doors and take us all down. Maybe—" Aus gasped. "He's still alive!" He turned back to Moe. "Open the door!"

But Jan lay still, an ever-growing pool of his own blood spreading beneath him. "Aus, ar—" Before William could finish, Jan twitched. "Shit! He is still alive."

The enemy had begun their charge, passing Jan and closing in on William and the others.

Aus grabbed the wheel to open the doors, but he halted. "It's too late, isn't it?" He returned to the window.

The army clearly thought Jan had passed, several of them jumping him, the soldiers directly behind them carrying the now-straightened tool to force the doors open. "I'm sorry, man." William put his hand on Aus' shoulder.

Jan raised his head and looked back at them. He pulled his coat open.

His voice hoarse, Aus said, "He was pretending to be dead."

"What?" William said.

Beneath his bulletproof vest, Jan wore two strings of cubes. They were smaller versions of the explosives that had lined the corridor. His body lit with a white flash. A clap ripped through the air.

The glow dazzled William, and the ground shook. Temporarily blinded, he rubbed his face. Aus hadn't moved. He cried without blinking.

The same scenes of charred carnage they'd left behind in the other section of corridor.

Piles of burned bodies.

Jan now one of them.

The walkie-talkie hissed, and Gracie said, "Aus? What's happening?"

William picked it up. "Gracie, this is William."

"What's happening, William? What was that sound?"

His sight returning, he peered through the glass. Diseased set upon those soldiers who remained, the explosion knocking down their shields. "The army's been stopped. We're okay on this side."

"And Dad?"

"I'm sorry, Gracie. I'm really sorry."

CHAPTER 35

The screams of men and women from the second hatch carried on the wind. Enough distance between him and them, Max strained to hear their shouted words. Not that he understood their language. The army clearly tried to coordinate against the attack, but a crowd that dense in such a confined space had no chance against a rapidly spreading disease. The bright flashes and cracks of bullet fire died down. Snarls and growls replaced them.

Why had they attacked Dout in the first place? Max hadn't wanted to kill them, but what else could he do? In a 'them or us' situation, it had to be them. Of course it had to be them. Especially as he was the one to blame for them being there.

And he'd beaten the diseased. They wouldn't control him anymore. At least something good had come from this. Now he could move on with the others. He wouldn't be the reason Olga got separated from her friends.

Max lifted his walkie-talkie, but before he pressed the button, something whispered through his skull, *Mad Max*.

"Huh?"

The creature stood about fifty feet away. A silhouette highlighted by the moon. It stared at him. It swayed with the long grass. Canted, one shoulder raised higher than the other. *Mad Max.*

"No!" Max pointed at the creature. "You won't do this to me anymore." His trousers were soaked with dew. His legs sore from the cold and damp fabric, he closed in on the diseased. "I won't be a slave to you. You won't bully me."

Mad Max.

Five feet away. The creature had long hair, but its emaciated form hid any visible signs of gender. Androgenised by infection. Its face changed. It morphed into his, "Mu—" No! Max stepped back. It wasn't his mum. He wouldn't call it that. A vile shell of a once-human, this creature had no kin. Its only connection to anything came from the shared bond of diseased blood.

Like his.

No. Not like his. He hadn't turned. He hadn't lost what made him human. Although, he had no way to physically connect to the girl he loved. He'd just driven the disease into hundreds of uninfected people. And he'd done it consciously. Did that make him worse than the unthinking creatures?

"I had to do that. They were going to kill the people I care about."

Mad—

"No!" His outburst spooked a flock of birds, and they burst from a nearby tree. Max stamped on the muddy ground. "Not again! This won't happen again. I won't be a slave to this anymore."

Mad Ma—

Max stepped so close to the creature their faces nearly touched. Deep cuts around its nose showed where it had been bitten. It reeked of the same vinegar tang of rotting flesh he knew oh so well. The thing also stank of shit like so many of them, their bodies emptying much like a corpse's would. "I won't be a slave to this. Say what you have to say."

The thing panted, its rancid breath pushing against his face. It stared at him with listless eyes. It stared through him.

"Just like I thought." Max shoved the creature. Its skinny arms flailed, and its twisted mouth stretched wide. It fell on its back with an "oomph." It twisted and turned, but remained where it had fallen. Why stand when it had nothing to attack? This creature, like every diseased he'd met, had but one purpose: to infect the world. When the opportunities to fulfil that purpose were gone—lying, standing, sitting ... what did it matter?

A gentle snarling and hissing from the creature on the ground, it stopped squirming and stared at the stars, lost in its own world. As a kid, Max had found his older brothers, Matthew and Greg, lying on the roof of their house in the summer. They were staring up at the night sky, giggling to one another. He must have been about ten at the time, and their behaviour had given him a strange feeling in his stomach. He cried to Drake about it, and it took for Sam to explain to him that his brothers had eaten some mushrooms that had done funny things to them. Matthew and Greg. His older brothers, they were close to adulthood, but they'd looked like children in that moment. Helpless, wide-eyed, vulnerable. The diseased he'd shoved over had that look. But, while it had that look, while it reminded him of the state he'd found his brothers in, and could have so easily morphed into them, it remained a pathetic diseased. Docile. Weak. And not the boss of him anymore. No Mad Max. No reminder of the scores of people he'd killed. No flashbacks to a lost life. Just a diseased. A weak and pathetic diseased.

It started low in his throat. A small laugh at first, Max's mirth grew louder until he threw his head back and howled at the sky. He pointed at the impotent creature. "You have no power over me. I don't have to hide away from you. You're not my mum and dad. You're not my brothers or any of the dead people I've known. You're pathetic. You're a slave to this hideous virus. You won't hold me back anymore. You won't prevent me living my life."

Max turned on his walkie-talkie. "Gracie, it's me, Max. Is Olg—"

"Oh, Max, I'm so glad to talk to you." Gracie's words were breathy as if she'd run a long distance.

"I had to turn my walkie-talkie off so I could sneak up on the two armies. I thought yo—"

"Two armies? Have you attacked them both?"

"Wasn't that the plan?"

"Oh no."

"What?"

"The diseased you loosed on the first army forced them down into the tunnel towards Dad, Aus, and the others."

"Which is what we wanted to happen, right?"

"Max?" Olga came through on the radio. She must have been with Gracie.

"Olga? What's going on? I don't understand what Gracie's saying."

"Jan's dead, Max. He died fighting the second wave driven into the tunnels by the diseased."

"And Artan and the others?"

"Did you send the diseased into their army?"

"Yes. That's what we agreed. Did I do the wrong thing?"

"No, you did what you thought was right. It would have been better if we'd held off a while, but you didn't know."

"But I still screwed up? I don't understand."

"You've done nothing wrong. We would have asked you to hold on had we spoken to you, but you did what we'd agreed. Look, Max, we need to keep the lines clear in case

Artan and the others need our help. We'll talk about this when we meet up."

The walkie-talkie fell silent. Max filled his lungs and rubbed his head. The creature he'd shoved over remained on the ground. It wore the same diseased face he'd been inches from. It snarled and twisted. No familiarity. No name-calling. He'd beaten his demons, but by sending the diseased into the second army, had he just killed his friends?

CHAPTER 36

Clang! The heavy metal shield hit the partly closed doors. Artan slipped through the gap and dragged it back with him. He raised his hand at Hawk and said, "That's enough!"

Hawk paused, his mouth open, his face glistening with sweat.

The walkie-talkie on Artan's hip sent out a burst of static, and Olga's voice came through. "We've finally spoken to Max. We didn't get to him in time. He's already sent the diseased over the barriers."

"Shit. Hawk"—Artan pointed at the other end of the long tunnel—"they're going to be on us any minute now."

While shaking his head, Hawk backed away from Artan. "I can't do half a job. There's only one more shield. This has to end now. Otherwise, what's the point?"

"The point is you stay alive. Isn't that fucking obvious?"

"That's not enough." Hawk shook his head and turned his back on them.

"I'll lock him in there if I need to," Freddie said. "We can't let this place fall because he wants to be a hero."

Thankfully, regardless of what Freddie said, Nick had taken control of the wheel. Artan shielded himself behind the half-closed door on the left and gripped his gun. He wouldn't follow Hawk, but he'd do everything he could to ensure he made it back.

Hawk ran over the scattered corpses with high steps.

Thud! A body fell through the hatch and landed on the cold steel. It lay still.

"Shit," Artan muttered, "that didn't take long."

Thud! Thud! Another two bodies. Even from this distance, the shock of their landing ran through the ground.

The next shield lay farther away than the first. About four hundred feet from where Artan stood.

The hatch rained soldiers. Many of them screamed as they fell. Every one fell silent when they landed.

"He has to come back," Freddie said.

Artan cupped his mouth with his hands. "Hawk, get back here, man. You can't do this."

Hawk acted like he hadn't heard him.

Thud-thud! Thud! Thud-thud-thud! While some soldiers fell, others climbed down the ladder. They slipped and scrambled in their haste to get away from what Max had set on them above.

The shield now about two hundred feet from Hawk.

Nick gasped.

Artan spun his way. "What? What is it?"

Nick's hand shook when he pointed down the corridor. One of the fallen soldiers clambered from the pile of bodies. "The corpses are softening their fall."

Artan cupped his mouth with his hands again. "Hawk! Look out."

Hawk arrived at the shield just as the first soldier climbing down the ladder reached the ground and joined his unsteady comrade.

Hawk dragged the shield back with him. It skimmed the tops of the burned corpses. It knocked heads and limbs from bodies.

The soldier on the ground aimed his gun at Hawk.

"Close those doors," Freddie said.

Artan shook his head. "Not yet. Hawk, watch your back. Use the shield! They're about to shoot!"

Hawk dragged the shield up over his back. He wore it like a shell. He lowered his head.

Artan tightened his grip on his gun, but with Hawk between them, he had no clear line of sight.

The *crack* of gunfire. The *ting* of bullets against Hawk's shield. Each shot shook Hawk. He stumbled once or twice.

Nick kept a hold of the wheel and leaned towards Artan. "If Hawk exposes himself for a second, they'll take his head off."

"I think he knows that," Artan said.

The closer Hawk got to the doors, the slower his pace. The heavy shield tore the black layer from the charred bodies, exposing the pink flesh beneath.

Freddie stepped closer to Nick and the wheel. "We have to close the door."

Artan shook his head. "I won't let him die."

"So you'll risk everyone's life in this place because your friend made an awful choice?"

"We're not at that point yet. He still has a chance."

"I wish I had your confidence."

"You don't need to wish for anything." Artan turned on Freddie and spoke through gritted teeth. "You just need to shut the fuck up."

Hawk tripped on a body and fell flat. There were about fifteen soldiers behind him now. All of them armed.

Artan pulled back as a stream of bullets flew down the tunnel. Some hit the steel door. Others flew past them through the gap. He returned fire. One short burst before Hawk clambered to his feet again.

One hundred and fifty feet away, Hawk's previously glistening face now dripped with sweat, and his pace had slowed to a walk.

"He won't make it. Nick," Freddie said, "close the door now! That's an order."

Nick continued to grip the wheel.

The army charged after Hawk. His shield sang with bullet fire. About one hundred feet from safety, the army was about three to four hundred feet behind him and closing in fast.

"I've had enough of this." Freddie shoved Nick aside and grabbed the wheel.

Artan slammed the butt of his gun into the side of Freddie's head. The bulky man's legs buckled, and he fell into a heap.

Nick stepped over him and gripped the wheel again. He held eye contact with Artan. "Just tell me when I need to close this door. I trust you."

The ringing of steel from bullet fire. The scrape from the shield dragging against the floor and walls. Hawk got to within twenty feet. The soldiers behind were about one hundred and fifty feet away.

His stomach tight, Artan fought against his own instincts. An army bearing down on them. They had to close the door. If they got in, the entire community would be screwed. But Hawk would make it.

"On the count of three," Artan said to Nick. He stood aside so Hawk could get through. He raised the barrel of his gun high so he could shoot over his head.

"One!"

Hawk ten feet away. The first wave of armed soldiers about one hundred feet behind. Many more were joining them as they jumped from the ladders.

"Two!"

Five feet.

"Three!"

Hawk stumbled through the gap, turned the shield sideways to bring it with him, and dropped it with a clattering clang.

Artan opened fire. The vibrations from his gun shook his entire upper body. The soldiers, a wall of flesh without protection, soaked up his attack. Many screamed as they fell.

Hawk grabbed a gun, jumped to his feet, and joined Artan at the closing gap in the doors.

The front row of soldiers down, those behind charged past.

The soldiers were now fifty feet away. The gap between the doors narrowed. Artan and Hawk attacked the front runners. But the front runners fought back.

A bullet slammed into the end of Artan's gun. Several more flew through the small gap and whizzed down the corridor.

The gap in the doors reduced to about two inches. Artan withdrew his weapon. Hawk did the same. Nick closed the doors.

All three of them panted, and Freddie groaned as he rolled on the ground.

"What happened to him?" Hawk said.

Artan shook his head. "I slipped and caught him with the end of my gun. Well done, Hawk."

The scarred hunter's eyes spread wide, and his cheeks bulged as he exhaled. "That was close, eh?"

"But worth it," Artan said.

"Look!" Nick pointed through the window in the steel doors.

Many of the soldiers continued to close in on them. One

of them held a large metal device. It narrowed to a paddle at the end.

"That must be what they used on the other side to force the doors open," Artan said.

Nick lifted a gun from the ground. "They're not getting in here."

"Lads," Hawk said, his face pressed so close to the window it steamed with his breaths, "I don't think we need to worry about them getting in."

The bodies that had rained down at the end of the tunnel had created a crash mat of human flesh. Soft enough to keep the fallen alive. But the fallen weren't soldiers anymore. Those at the top of the heap twitched and twisted. They snapped and snarled. They scrambled to their feet. They slashed at the air. They charged at the soldiers.

"You think they can beat the diseased?" Nick said.

Artan shook his head while the soldiers opened fire. "No." A stream of diseased rained through the hatch. "They'll run out of ammo before they kill them all. And even if they don't, we'll finish them off when they come through. They don't have their shields anymore."

The wave of diseased flooded forwards.

The soldiers ran towards the closed doors. Several of them slammed their hands against the steel and pressed their faces to the glass. They might have spoken a language Artan didn't recognise, but he recognised fear. He recognised cries for help. Artan's stomach tied in knots. He wouldn't wish this on anyone.

The man on the other side of the glass barked words Artan didn't understand, but Artan maintained eye contact. The man shouted and screamed. He snarled and hissed. His glare turned from brown to crimson. He bit at the air between them as if his sheer will to pass on his new affliction would somehow surpass the very real barrier of steel and reenforced glass.

Artan's shoulders slumped. He released a hard sigh. A hand slipped into his. He turned to the smiling Nick.

"You made the right call," Nick said.

Heat smothered Artan's cheeks. He nodded.

"You know"—Hawk cocked his head to one side—"I'm pleased I didn't get selected to run with Aus' team."

"Really?" Artan said.

Hawk pointed at Artan and Nick. "This wouldn't have happened had I gone in your place."

"No." Artan smiled at Nick. "It probably wouldn't."

Freddie sat up and held the welt on the side of his face. He glared at Artan. But then he looked at Hawk and the two shields. The locked steel doors. The bleeding eyeballs staring through the glass at them.

"Look," Artan said, "I'm sorry, but if we'd closed the doors and left the shields in there with them, they'd have defended against the diseased and forced the doors open. They and the diseased would have swarmed this place."

While opening and closing his jaw as if testing it still worked, Freddie nodded. "I can't say I'm happy about what just happened, but I understand."

An aggressive static hiss from where he pressed the button on his walkie-talkie, Artan said, "Olga, we've secured this side. What now?"

"It's over, Artan," Olga said.

"What?"

"We've beaten them. For now. The only thing left for us to do is leave. Dout's cover has been blown. It's only a matter of time before they attack again. Max is making sure the end of the escape tunnel is clear before we evacuate. Good job, you've bought us the time we need to get out of here. See you in the pleasure dome."

CHAPTER 37

William's elbows throbbed and stung from where he'd dragged himself on his stomach for close to two miles. He'd travelled most of the length of the steel escape tunnel, through the funky reek of over two hundred bodies that had gone before him. His clothes clung to his sweat-damp body, restricting his movements when he climbed from the end of the escape hatch. He filled his lungs with the fresher outside air. The wind dried his sweating skin. Matilda on his heels, he reached down to her and helped her climb out.

Dried sweat and the sun's bright glare combined, searing his tired eyes. He'd not slept for over twenty-four hours, and he wouldn't anytime soon. But they'd made it. All of them had made it.

Surrounded by people from Dout, it took William a few seconds to locate Max. He stood about one hundred feet away near a mound of fallen diseased.

"There are far fewer of them than I expected," Matilda said.

William said, "Our plan clearly worked. The two armies must have pulled them away from here. Although …"

"With how they pump people out of those gates, it won't be long before more arrive."

"Exactly," William said. "And if we're still with all the people from Dout, will they expect us to fight for them again? I know that sounds harsh, but we didn't sign up for this. We've done more than enough already."

Matilda held her bottom lip in a pinch. "We need to get out of here before we have to make that choice. Also, I'm tired of this sausage fest. I'm not sure they have it in them to work out women can fight too. And I've not got the energy to educate them."

Artan emerged from the crowd of people. He wrapped Matilda in a tight hug. He then grabbed William and said, "I'm glad you're both okay."

"And you, man."

Nick and Hawk close by, Olga brought Max over a second later.

"You should have seen Hawk," Artan said.

The scowl Hawk had worn for the past few days had finally lifted. He shrugged. "Anyone would have done the same had they thought of it."

William smiled. "We heard it on the walkie-talkie. So you went back for the shields while the army came down on you?"

Hawk snorted. "I'm not stupid." He shook his head. "I went back for the shields, and *then* the army came down on us. I was all in at that point, so I saw it out. In fact, I needed the shield to cover my arse while I ran away from them."

"He's underplaying what he did," Artan said. "It was epic, and he's the reason we're here now." He reached out and took Nick's hand, turning to Matilda. "Nick's coming with us, if that's okay?"

If anyone else had an opinion on it, Artan clearly didn't care. Matilda smiled like she hadn't for a very long time. An infectious smile that William caught. Any fog from the past few days got burned away by the brilliance of her joy. She nodded. "Yes! Yes, of course it is."

All the while, Max had stood at the edge of the group, avoiding eye contact. "Max," William said, "you saved us. Thank you."

Max shook his head. "I—"

"Look around." William swept his arm out to show Max their surroundings and the people gathered there. "These people are alive because of *you*."

Max frowned hard, as if trying to make sense of his own thoughts.

Aus and Freddie appeared. Freddie had a red mark and swelling on one side of his face. "What happened to you?" William said.

"I'm sorry," Artan said. "I panicked, and—"

"It's fine," Freddie said. "You did what had to be done. Had I closed the doors on Hawk, we'd still be fighting in Dout."

"And, Max ..." Aus said.

Max stepped away from the volatile man.

Aus cleared his throat. "I got you wrong. I'm sorry. Were you not here, we would have fallen to that attack. We all owe you our lives."

The frown on Max's face deepened. He shook his head and said, "No. I don't—"

Dianna arrived, cutting him off. Before William could ask where she'd been for most of their time in Dout, Gracie also appeared. Pale, she had dark bags beneath her bloodshot eyes. She clapped her hands once and said, "People of Dout, many of us have made it here, and I'm sure many of you are scared. Scared about what the future holds. What kind of life we can have after Dout. How we will stay safe. But before we turn our attention to the future, I want us to look at the past. At the people who have fallen, not just in this battle, but all of those who have left us while Dout was our home. This is a new era." Her voice wavered. "And our leader's gone. There are lots of questions and uncertainties, so I ask you all for patience and support while we try to get everything in order. The primary concern for now is everyone's safety. We need to move on soon. We'll work out a plan and put it to you when we have one."

While Gracie spoke, Max shook his head repeatedly and rocked where he stood. As much as William had wanted to hear what Gracie said, Max's increasing display of distress took his focus. Even Gracie threw several glances at him during her speech.

William put his arm around Max and led him away. "It's okay, mate. We're going to get through this. You're over the worst of it, and you've faced your fears. You've come outside. You're the reason so many people have survived."

But Max wore a vacant glaze. He rocked and shook his head as if he'd erupt with the energy building inside him.

Olga and Matilda came over. Artan, Nick, and Hawk. Dianna and then Gracie, her face twisted, she chewed on her bottom lip. What had gone on between them? What did she know that the others didn't? Whatever it was, judging by Max's behaviour, they were all about to find out.

CHAPTER 38

Max sneered. What did William know? Sure, he wanted him to feel better, but he didn't know the truth.

William looked him in the eyes. "You saved everyone, Max. Remember that. This community owes you their lives."

Their lives wouldn't have been at risk were it not for him.

"Do you need to sit down?" William said. Matilda appeared beside him. Artan, Nick, Hawk, Dianna, Olga.

Not even Olga knew what he'd done.

"Is everything okay, Max?" Gracie said, her pale skin now shock white. Her lips were tight. "Are you all right?"

In other words, keep your fucking mouth shut!

"Everything's done now," Gracie said. "It's over. We need to move on, and we need to do it soon."

Move on and live with the fact that Dout fell because *he'd* screwed up. And he'd judged Hugh for what he'd done back in Edin. His family had died because of Hugh. Gracie had lost her dad because of him.

"You need to take some time to let the dust settle," Gracie said. "Try not to let everything overwhelm you."

"This is bullshit, Gracie."

William and Matilda were the closest to Max. His outburst drove them back several steps.

"You know that more than anyone."

Olga looked between Gracie and Max. "What's he talking about?"

"I just wanted to feel better," Max said. "I could see how much of a liability I was, and I wanted to feel better so we could move on. Oh, Olga." His vision of her blurred through his tears. "I could see you didn't want to stay in Dout, and I didn't want to be the reason for your unhappiness."

Louder than before, Olga shook when she said, "What's going on?"

"Isn't it obvious?" Max said.

"Max!" Gracie said.

Max pointed his thumb at his chest. "*I* was the one who gave away Dout's location."

"*What?*" Dianna said. "This happened because of *you?*"

Olga turned on Dianna. "Shut up!" And then back to Max. "What on earth are you talking about?"

Gracie cleared her throat and kept her voice low. "I don't think we need to tell the entire community about this. Olga, remember when you saw Max after we'd been together and he'd had a shower?"

A tightened jaw, Olga's nostrils flared.

"I found him after he'd been outside. He'd been mixing with the diseased."

"I wanted to get over my fear of them."

"He left the hatch open and paid no attention to whether he might be seen or not. It was all on camera."

"Someone saw him?" Olga said.

Gracie sighed and scratched her head. "I thought I saw someone outside, watching from the shadows. I couldn't be sure until the two armies arrived."

"What happened to the footage?"

"I could see he wasn't himself. And, were it not for him, I wouldn't be here now. I'd still be in the Asylum. I covered up for him." Tears shimmered in her green eyes. The others watched her with confused frowns. She sighed and spoke to the ground. "I deleted the footage showing what he'd done and hoped it wouldn't come back to haunt us."

CHAPTER 39

Artan's jaw fell. Max had blown Dout's cover? All of this had happened because of him? "Wh—? Why? Ho—?" Did it need explaining any more than that? Max had well and truly screwed up, and Gracie had covered for him. "Bu—"

It happened so fast it took Artan a second to catch up. Aus came in from the right, tackled Max around the waist, and slammed him to the ground. Max wheezed from where the weight of the large man landed on top of him.

Artan charged Aus. William, Hawk, and Matilda also closed in on him. A monster of a man, Aus kicked and writhed, but they overpowered him and pulled him free.

The blade in Aus' hand caught the light. Blood dripped from it. Max remained on his back, his hands clasped to his stomach.

"Max!" Olga's shriek ran across the meadow.

Gracie hit Aus like he'd hit Max, and they both went down. Her teeth clenched, she punched her brother square in the face. "Why would you do that?" She punched him again and again, each blow landing with the wet crunch of breaking cartilage. "Why?"

Artan stepped forwards, but Nick held onto him. "Leave it. These two have needed to have this confrontation ever since I've known them."

When Aus, while under attack from his sister, threw his knife to one side, Artan relaxed.

Aus flipped Gracie onto her back and pinned her by her shoulders. Blood dripped from his mouth, and he spoke with a slur. "You knew he'd been outside."

"I didn't know he'd given away Dout's location."

"But you thought he might have?" Aus sprayed a red mist of spittle. "And you didn't think it might be a good idea to warn us? You put us all in danger. Dad *died* because of you."

A sharp twist, Gracie slipped from beneath Aus. She pulled his right arm and used the momentum of his fall to send him crashing into the ground while she mounted him again.

Artan's friends tended to Max. Most of Aus' crew had come to Aus' side while he fought his sister. Artan could do nothing to help anyone.

"You've always been an arsehole to me, Aus. All I remember is you being mean." She looked up at his crew. "And it's only me. These people love you. I don't." She shook her head. "I allowed it because of Dad, but now he's gone, there's no reason for me to lie. I fucking *hate* you." She lifted him by his shirt and slammed him back down against the ground. "I hate you!"

There were no diseased in their vicinity, but if Gracie didn't calm down, there would be soon. Of the few people gathered around, none of them looked willing to intervene. Artan stepped closer just as Gracie quietened.

Her frame slumped. Her voice weary, she said, "And I don't get it. I never have. You were *always* Dad's favourite, so why did you hate me so much?"

Just like the daylight had caught the glint of Aus' blade, it caught the glisten in his watery eyes. His thick jaw trembled, and his usually booming voice lost its resonance. It came out as a thin and reedy rasp. "Because Mum loved you more."

Gracie sagged but remained on top of her brother. "What are you talking about? I was five when she died. I barely remember her."

"I do." Aus paused, and his tears broke, running down either side of his face. His glazed eyes flicked from one of hers to the other. "I remember how she sang to you. How she carried you around the house the entire time. Like she—" his deep inhale lifted and lowered Gracie with the expansion and contraction of his diaphragm "—never wanted to let you go."

All the while, Gracie shook her head. She frowned. Her eyes glistened.

"You two were inseparable," Aus said. "She was always too busy for me." He clenched his trembling jaw. The thunder returned to his voice. "Because of *you*, I didn't have enough time with my mum."

Gracie shook her head. "I didn't make her ill."

"No, but you stole every chance I had to be close to her. You lost Mum when you were five. I lost her when you were born. Imagine what that loss must feel like. She's right in front of you, but she's already gone."

Lifting him by his shirt again, Gracie slammed him against the hard ground. "You think I don't know about loss?"

"She died twice for me, Gracie. And no matter how hard I've tried to feel different, I will *forever* hate you for that."

Gracie slammed him down again. His head hit the hard ground with a hollow knock. "I was a kid." She slammed him again. And again. "You punished me because of her behaviour." Another hard slam, Aus' eyes rolled in his head. "I needed you. I needed Dad. You say I don't know how it feels, but you were Dad's favourite, and you *had* him."

Aus spoke with a slur. "And you took him away from me too."

"Yeargh!"

Artan noticed the rock beneath Aus' head too late. As Gracie slammed him down one last time, something cracked. Artan's stomach flipped when Aus' head rolled to one side.

Gracie stood up and stumbled back. Her face shock white, she cried with unblinking eyes.

Freddie had already dropped and had two fingers along Aus' neck to feel for a pulse. He slumped and shook his head.

Gracie stood alone. Her hands balled at her sides. Her glazed stare fixed on her dead brother.

"Grac—"

"Give her a minute," Nick said.

It had all happened so fast. The minutes had passed like seconds. His friends remained around the downed Max. Artan walked over to Matilda and rested a hand on her back. "Is he okay?"

Matilda stepped aside.

Olga kneeled beside Max, his head in her hands. Max stared up at her through eyes that were finally his own. The torment had gone. The weight of responsibility had lifted.

William applied pressure to Max's wound, and Hawk tore his shirt into strips for bandages. Artan couldn't do anything more to help.

Freddie, who'd remained at Aus' side, got to his feet and stepped away from his dead friend. Dianna stood beside him.

Artan shook his head and pointed at her. "You!"

"What?" Dianna said. Her fists balled; her shoulders squared.

"You're a fucking snake."

Dianna's lips peeled back. "I don't want to be around

people like *you* lot. When we were walking through the ruined city, Hawk put us in danger every chance he could. And now Max has toppled an entire community."

Wildfire burned in Olga's glare, and she snarled at the girl.

"Freddie's going to take the people of Dout away from here to find somewhere else to live," Dianna said. "We're going to go north where it's quieter."

"We should have left you in the asylum," Matilda said.

Aus dead on the ground, Max bleeding out while Olga held him. Yet Dianna still pushed her lips together like a smug child. "But you didn't, did you? And now I'm done with you and your insanity. I'm leaving with Freddie."

Freddie turned to Dianna. "We don't want you."

"What? After the information I just gave you?"

"And what did that information lead to?" He wrapped his large hand around the back of Dianna's head and forced her to look at the dead Aus. He then turned her towards Max. "And look! How have you helped anyone? We don't want someone like you with us."

"But—"

"Looks like you're on your own," Artan said.

Dianna looked from Freddie to the downed Max.

"I didn't mean for this—"

"Fuck. Off," Freddie said.

"Bu—"

"Now!"

Dianna held her ground for another few seconds before she walked away from the group.

Freddie's gaze fell on Max. He sighed, shook his head, and walked off in a different direction, his crew going with him. Nick remained at Artan's side.

"You still want to come with us?" Artan said.

Nick put his arm around him and kissed the top of his

head. "Always."

Max's moment of peace had gone. His face red. His eyes bulged. His mouth stretched wide while he gasped.

Olga sobbed over him. "I'm so sorry, Max. I didn't see him coming. Hold on, you'll be fine. We'll get help."

But William had taken the pressure from Max's wound, and Hawk had stopped tearing bandage strips.

"What are you both doing?" Olga said. "Get back into Dout. There must be something in there that can help."

William cried freely. "You need to make the most of this time, Olga." He got to his feet and stepped away.

"No!" Olga said. "Help him! You *have* to."

Reaching up with a shaking hand, Max touched the side of Olga's face. He spoke with a whisper. "I wouldn't change a thing."

Sobs ran through Olga in waves.

Serenity returned to Max's fading stare. The Max Artan had only seen glimpses of. The Max Matilda had told him she knew from national service. The Max who still had a mum, dad, and brothers at home. The one who hadn't killed hundreds of diseased. Who hadn't borne the weight of his friends' lives on his weary shoulders.

"I finally get to be with my family," Max said. "And when your time comes, I'll be waiting."

Olga's reply ripped Artan's stomach out. "I'll come with you now."

Max shook his head. "It's not your time."

Holding his face in her hands, Olga leaned closer to Max.

Artan, Matilda, and William all shouted, "*No!*"

A slight pause, Olga turned to her friends. "I need this. I know what it'll do to me, but I need this more than anything. Just make sure you kill me when I turn."

Too far away, Artan managed one step towards Olga before she kissed Max.

CHAPTER 40

William had brought a sword with him from Gracie's community. He held it at arm's length in his shaking hand. Just pointing it at his hunched friend went against his every instinct, and the Olga he knew would have cut his throat for the gesture. But she simply sat there, holding Max's head, leaning over him, staring into his dead eyes.

Matilda, Hawk, Artan, and Nick all stood with similar weapons. Freddie and the others had taken all the guns and ammo, and none of them had the strength for an argument. Hopefully, where they were going, they didn't need guns.

Tears stood in Matilda's eyes. Other than Max, she was closer to Olga than anyone. Whatever happened, he couldn't expect her to do it. Hopefully Nick would recognise his place in the group. The one with the least attachment. He should step up and do what needed to be done.

"H-how long do we wait?" Hawk said.

A few minutes had passed. How long did they wait? William offered his best guess. He shrugged.

The slightest snarl. The clearing of a throat. William should lunge at Olga now, but he froze. And a good job too.

The Olga who looked up didn't have a layer of blood coating her eyes. Max, on the other hand...

"Get back!" William said.

But Olga didn't move.

Were they standing toe to toe, Olga would have kicked his arse. William shoved her away just as Max snarled and sat up.

It turned William's stomach to plunge the end of his sword into Max's face. The tip burst from the back of his friend's head.

His grip weak, William let go, and his sword fell with Max's slumped body.

Standing over his fallen friend, William released a hard sigh. What must it have been like for him to kill his entire family? "I hope I never have to do that again."

Olga remained on her back several feet away. Her features wavered between rage and regret.

Weaponless, William waited.

Olga said, "So what are you going to do? Are you going to end me or what? I'm okay if you want to cut me down now and be done with it."

Hawk cleared his throat with a cough. "I think she would have turned by now. Maybe we keep our distance and remain vigilant for a bit longer, but eventually, if she doesn't turn, we have to accept she won't."

Olga stared into the middle distance and said, "Or you could just end me now."

∽

FREDDIE HAD TAKEN the residents of Dout and moved on. Gracie remained nearby. She sat on her own, away from the group. "If there are any diseased in the area," William said to the others, "I think they'll be following Freddie and his lot.

And they have enough people to defend against an attack. But we can't stay here forever. We have to move on soon. It seems pretty clear Olga won't turn."

"The worst of it," Olga said—she'd barely moved since William had shoved her over—"is that Max and I could have had what we wanted, but we played it safe." She spoke from behind an invisible wall that had slammed down in front of her since Max passed. Her eyes were glazed and unfocused. Her words floated as if coming from a dream. "We held each other when we slept in the same bed, but we never took it any further. We never kissed until now. And maybe that's all we could have done. Maybe the infection would have spread in other ways, but even that—" She lost her words. A fresh wave of tears ran down her cheeks. She coughed several times. "That would have been so much more than what we allowed ourselves." Her words trailed off when she said, "That would have been enough."

The scuffing of feet nearby, William jumped and spun around to find Gracie, washed out and with bloodshot eyes. She fixed on Olga and whispered, "I'm so, so sorry."

Olga pursed her lips and flicked her head toward the fallen Aus. "Me too."

Gracie lingered for a moment and said, "Can I come with you?"

For the first time since Max had died, Olga nodded and smiled. Brief, but her spirit shone through. "Yes. Of course you can." Her grief closed in again.

Artan stepped forwards while holding Nick's hand. "Uh," he said, "we think we've worked out a way to get over the wall."

END OF BOOK NINE.

Thank you for reading *Before the Dawn:* Book nine of Beyond These Walls.

The Wall: Book Ten of Beyond These Walls is available now - Go to www.michaelrobertson.co.uk

Have you checked out *Fury:* Book one in Tales from beyond These Walls? It's a standalone story set in the city of Fury. While it can be read independently of the main Beyond These Walls series, and features new characters, the story occurs at the same time as Between Fury and Fear: Book eight of Beyond These Walls.

If you're yet to read it, go to www.michaelrobertson.co.uk to check out *Fury:* Book one in Tales from Beyond These Walls.

Support The Author

Dear reader, as an independent author I don't have the resources of a huge publisher. If you like my work and would like to see more from me in the future, there are two things you can do to help: leaving a review, and a word-of-mouth referral.

Releasing a book takes many hours and hundreds of dollars. I love to write, and would love to continue to do so. All I ask is that you leave an Amazon review. It shows other readers that you've enjoyed the book and will encourage them to give it a try too. The review can be just one sentence, or as long as you like.

If you've enjoyed Beyond These Walls, you might also enjoy my other post-apocalyptic series. The Alpha Plague: Books 1-8 (The Complete Series) are available now.

The Alpha Plague - Available Now - Go to www.michaelrobertson.co.uk

Or save money by picking up the entire series box set.

ABOUT THE AUTHOR

Like most children born in the seventies, Michael grew up with Star Wars in his life, along with other great stories like Labyrinth, The Neverending Story, and as he grew older, the Alien franchise. An obsessive watcher of movies and consumer of stories, he found his mind wandering to stories of his own.

Those stories had to come out.

He hopes you enjoy reading his work as much as he does creating it.

Contact
www.michaelrobertson.co.uk
subscribers@michaelrobertson.co.uk

READER GROUP

Join my reader group for all my latest releases and special offers. You'll also receive these four FREE books. You can unsubscribe at any time.

Go to - www.michaelrobertson.co.uk

THE ARENA
MICHAEL ROBERTSON

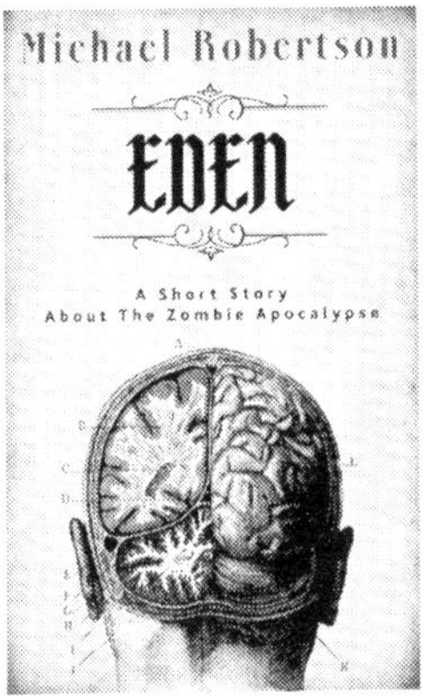
Michael Robertson
EDEN
A Short Story
About The Zombie Apocalypse

RAT RUN
A POST-APOCALYPTIC TALE
Michael Robertson

ALSO BY MICHAEL ROBERTSON

THE SHADOW ORDER:

The Shadow Order

The First Mission - Book Two of The Shadow Order

The Crimson War - Book Three of The Shadow Order

Eradication - Book Four of The Shadow Order

Fugitive - Book Five of The Shadow Order

Enigma - Book Six of The Shadow Order

Prophecy - Book Seven of The Shadow Order

The Faradis - Book Eight of The Shadow Order

The Complete Shadow Order Box Set - Books 1 - 8

∿

NEON HORIZON:

The Blind Spot - A Cyberpunk Thriller - Neon Horizon Book One.

Prime City - A Cyberpunk Thriller - Neon Horizon Book Two.

Bounty Hunter - A Cyberpunk Thriller - Neon Horizon Book Three.

Connection - A Cyberpunk Thriller - Neon Horizon Book Four.

Reunion - A Cyberpunk Thriller - Neon Horizon Book Five.

Neon Horizon - Books 1 - 3 Box Set - A Science Fiction Thriller.

∿

THE ALPHA PLAGUE:

The Alpha Plague: A Post-Apocalyptic Action Thriller

The Alpha Plague 2

The Alpha Plague 3

The Alpha Plague 4

The Alpha Plague 5

The Alpha Plague 6

The Alpha Plague 7

The Alpha Plague 8

The Complete Alpha Plague Box Set - Books 1 - 8

∿

BEYOND THESE WALLS:

Protectors - Book one of Beyond These Walls

National Service - Book two of Beyond These Walls

Retribution - Book three of Beyond These Walls

Collapse - Book four of Beyond These Walls

After Edin - Book five of Beyond These Walls

Three Days - Book six of Beyond These Walls

The Asylum - Book seven of Beyond These Walls

Between Fury and Fear - Book eight of Beyond These Walls

Before the Dawn - Book nine of Beyond These Walls

The Wall - Book ten of Beyond These Walls

Beyond These Walls - Books 1 - 6 Box Set

∿

TALES FROM BEYOND THESE WALLS:

Fury - Book one of Tales From Beyond These Walls

∿

OFF-KILTER TALES:

The Girl in the Woods - A Ghost's Story - Off-Kilter Tales Book One

Rat Run - A Post-Apocalyptic Tale - Off-Kilter Tales Book Two

∾

Masked - A Psychological Horror

∾

CRASH:

Crash - A Dark Post-Apocalyptic Tale

Crash II: Highrise Hell

Crash III: There's No Place Like Home

Crash IV: Run Free

Crash V: The Final Showdown

∾

NEW REALITY:

New Reality: Truth

New Reality 2: Justice

New Reality 3: Fear

∾

Audiobooks:

CLICK HERE TO VIEW MY FULL AUDIOBOOK LIBRARY.

Printed in Great Britain
by Amazon